Everything inside the room was in disarray—it looked as if a tornado had blown through it. I saw books strewn everywhere. Hundreds of books, many on the floor beside overturned cartons, their covers flung wide, the dust jackets entirely or partially off, their pages spread facedown on the floor.

The room had been ransacked. Somebody had come in and taken it apart. From wall to wall, and corner to corner. *But for what reason?*

I reached shakily for the cell phone clipped to the waist of my jeans, punched in 911, and waited.

The operator came on after a couple of rings. "Hello, what's your emergency?"

I was about to tell her when I heard an engine revving to life behind me.

"Please tell me the emergency," the operator repeated.

I didn't say anything. Stunned and confused by that sound, I turned my head and stared out toward the end of the building, where I'd left my Toyota with the keys hanging in the ignition. . . .

Turned in time to see the SUV tear out of the facility's lot and onto the road, then speed off into the gathering dusk with a loud screech of tires.

"Hello, if someone's on the line, I need you to tell me the emergency!" the 911 operator was insisting urgently.

I opened my mouth, shut it, opened it again.

"Somebody just stole my vehicle."

SCENE
OF THE GRIME

A GRIME SOLVERS MYSTERY

Suzanne Price

A SIGNET BOOK

SIGNET
Published by New American Library, a division of
Penguin Group (USA) Inc., 375 Hudson Street,
New York, New York 10014, USA
Penguin Group (Canada), 90 Eglinton Avenue East, Suite 700, Toronto,
Ontario M4P 2Y3, Canada (a division of Pearson Penguin Canada Inc.)
Penguin Books Ltd., 80 Strand, London WC2R 0RL, England
Penguin Ireland, 25 St. Stephen's Green, Dublin 2,
Ireland (a division of Penguin Books Ltd.)
Penguin Group (Australia), 250 Camberwell Road, Camberwell, Victoria 3124,
Australia (a division of Pearson Australia Group Pty. Ltd.)
Penguin Books India Pvt. Ltd., 11 Community Centre, Panchsheel Park,
New Delhi - 110 017, India
Penguin Group (NZ), 67 Apollo Drive, Rosedale, North Shore,
Auckland 1311, New Zealand (a division of Pearson New Zealand Ltd.)
Penguin Books (South Africa) (Pty.) Ltd., 24 Sturdee Avenue,
Rosebank, Johannesburg 2196, South Africa

Penguin Books Ltd., Registered Offices:
80 Strand, London WC2R 0RL, England

First published by Signet, an imprint of New American Library,
a division of Penguin Group (USA) Inc.

First Printing, June 2007
10 9 8 7 6 5 4 3 2 1

Copyright © Penguin Group (USA) Inc., 2007
All rights reserved

Ⓟ REGISTERED TRADEMARK—MARCA REGISTRADA

For our dear friends
Ohrvel and Carol Carlson,
without whom there would be
no Pigeon Cove

SCENE OF THE GRIME

Chapter 1

I was crouched on an expensive Oriental rug under an antique walnut table outside Mr. Monahan's room, thinking. That's normal for me, though there are variations—it isn't like I'm neurotic about sticking to a set routine.

A few for instances: Sometimes I'll work my way deep into a kitchen cupboard before I start thinking in earnest. Other times I'll get to thinking under a mountain of dirty dishes. I have had decent thoughts in dusty parlors, and I've had thoughts that would pay off big-time while hovering over an ironing board in a steamy laundry room. Some of my *best* thinking ever has been done on ladders and stepstools under thirsty hanging plants, or even kneeling on floor tiles near a claw-foot tub. Usually I've got a mop, spray bottle, feather duster, and one of my handy-dandy all-purpose bamboo skewers within reach, but these are open to substitution. The only constant is my cleaning supplies kit. Believe it or not, I don't think I could get any thinking done without it. More friend and partner than accessory, the kit is my version of Felix the Cat's bag of tricks. It's here for me to reach into whenever I get in a fix, and it's one of the few things I've kept from my old life in New York. But then, my late husband bought it for me as a birthday gift the year we were married. Because of its practicality—or maybe I should say because it reminds me that Paul, who was the world's biggest dreamer, was never too lost in the clouds to appreciate my obsession with the practical, a foreign quality to him before we met—I treasure it more than all the jewelry and expensive perfume he gave on other occasions. It was his way of showing he loved me for everything I was, including my persnickety habits when it came to order and tidiness. And though people sometimes shoot me weird looks once they realize how much I cherish it, you can bet they aren't my close friends—or even casual ones.

The point is, anybody who knows me at all could figure that cleaning kit would be one of the items I'd want to keep forever. And those who would argue that I'm rigid in my behavior don't really understand, or care to understand, what makes me tick. One thing I've learned since Paul died is that I adjust pretty well.

Yes, Sky Taylor can bend a whole lot of different ways before she breaks. I'm just uncompromisingly clean, and that tends to bug certain people.

On the other hand, Abel Monahan, sweetheart

that he was, probably appreciated it about me more than anyone in the world. You could say he was a kindred spirit when it came to meticulousness, and hearing scuttlebutt that he'd checked in at the Millwood B&B was the main reason I'd stayed up half the night to get a jump on my newspaper column—when Old Abe was around, I cleared as much time as possible for hanging out with him. This was in direct contrast to my desire to avoid the Slobby Bunch down the hall, though they'd already put their nasty personal stamp on my morning. But I didn't want to fume about them, or the half-chewed Gummi Bear one of the kids—at least I *hope* it wasn't Mom or Dad—had left stuck on the Soumak rug like goopy raspberry red roadkill.

Old Abe, as we affectionately called him in Pigeon Cove, had been a regular guest at the inn for over a decade, visiting about five or six times a year and always booking the same upstairs room for his weeklong stays. I didn't know many specifics about Old Abe's life outside our little Cape Ann tourist hamlet, besides the fact that he had a home a few thousand miles south, in Florida. For all the hours we spent talking together, he never mentioned what he'd done for a living before retirement, or whether he'd been married, or had kids, or grandkids, or any living relatives. He never spoke about his past, or said where he'd been born and raised, though every now and then his pronunciations would say "Chicago" to me. I didn't push to find out if my guess was right;

people are entitled to share what they want with others, and keep the rest to themselves.

Besides, Old Abe had enough to say without my feeding him topics of conversation. He was an expert on classic American architecture, an interest I supposed might have first attracted him to the Cove. He liked talking books, often while showing off the twenty-five- and fifty-cent bargains he'd picked up at library and yard sales. He enjoyed vegetable gardening and could tell a perfect tomato at a glance. He *loved* to chat about the ins and outs of his favorite diversion, which was building a dry stone wall on a little wooded plot he owned south of town.

And, oh, have I mentioned that I loved to listen to him?

It's why I'd gotten to the Millwood a little before nine a.m. for my professional housecleaning rounds—that's right, *housecleaning*; no shame, writing freelance pieces for a small-circulation paper doesn't pay the bills—still bleary-eyed from hours of typing away at the computer. Margaret Millwood, sole proprietor of the inn, is known hither and yon for her scrumptious breakfast buffets, served promptly to guests at nine o'clock sharp every morning. So when my friend, landlord, and slightly crazed life coach Chloe Edwards told me she'd seen Old Abe roll into town for the Memorial Day weekend, I decided to head out early and say hello to him before getting to work.

Unfortunately, things hadn't worked out as planned. As I pulled my Toyota RAV4 into the inn's little parking area, I didn't notice Old Abe's battered Ford, and wondered if Chloe had been mistaken about the one she'd seen being his. But Marge had confirmed that Mr. Monahan had, in fact, arrived the night before.

"He must've decided to go straight out to that scrub lot of his," she'd said with a frown, shaking her head hard enough to wobble its netted mound of blue-gray hair. Marge considered it a slight if someone skipped her patented breakfasts. "Car's been gone since I woke up. Building a wall out of rocks in the middle of all that tangled brush . . . he says it relaxes him, can you imagine?"

Actually, I could, my disappointment aside. I like figuring things out, especially things other people can't. And I was sort of fascinated by the idea of patiently fitting all those loose stones together as if they were pieces of a scrambled natural puzzle.

But that was beside the point. Mr. Monahan had been building a freestanding stone wall for years out of rocks he gathered from local beaches, or dug up while planting his little vegetable patches in the lot. Though it was a crisp, bright May morning, the local forecast called for rain later on, and listening to WBZ-AM in my RAV4 I'd heard it was already pouring around Boston, just thirty or forty miles south of us on Route 128. If Old Abe meant to make any headway today, it made sense that he'd try and beat the wet weather moving up the coast.

But I wasn't going to argue with Marge, who

was as crusty and hardheaded a New Englander as I'd met. Instead, I hefted my cleaning kit over my shoulder and went upstairs to start on my mission. My uniform attire, as usual, consisted of one of my funky, freaky-deaky, former-eighties-rock-star-costume-designer mother's silk-screened tattoo blouses, a pair of black parachute pants with lots of functional patch pockets and hidden pouches, and distressed poppy red Keds slip-ons.

Incidentally, the best way I could've described Mom's latest couturial masterpiece to arrive in the mail—and for the record, it was white, and not flesh-colored like the racier version she would wear without any shame—would have been to say it showed something resembling a purple moon orchid wrapped in what might have been a winged, multicolored serpent, with an exploding rainbow in the background. If you're getting the idea that I share her eye for wildly colorful clothes, you're right on. The more vibrant, the better. Sometimes I think it shows an aspect of my personality that wouldn't be revealed any other way . . . a part of me I'm not sure even *I* know all that well, and that maybe intimidates me just a bit.

Okay, end of discussion. I'm scaring myself.

As I reached the second floor, I knew it would be one of those days. Marge had given me fair notice about the Slobby Bunch, jabbing her chin in their direction as they clomped down to the buffet in their soiled work shoes and sneakers, so I fully expected their room to be turned inside out. I hadn't, however, figured they'd leave the outer *hall* in need of major disaster relief. There were crumpled candy wrappers on the stairs and landing, half-filled soda glasses on the corner stands, muddy heel marks tracking to and from their door—and worst of all, under the edge of the walnut table, there was that Gummi Bear on Marge's prized Persian rug. The very same rug she'd often told me was woven by an armless nun in a remote eighteenth-century Turkish monastery, pointing to the tiny, perfectly round hole in the middle as proof.

"The sister used her toes to spin the rug, and that's where she'd sit when she worked on it," Marge would insist.

Yes, I know, it sounded like the real spinning had been done by a clever salesman working on Marge's trustful nature. But fact or fancy, it increased the value of the rug for her. And as I stood upstairs staring at it, I was only grateful that her arthritic knees and hips kept her from going upstairs much.

Then I started to think about how I'd get the chewy mess off of it.

Setting aside my bag of tricks, I hunkered down to inspect it and had my fears confirmed—the gum was still soft. That meant I would need to harden it before making any attempt at removal; otherwise it would just stick to the fibers in little clots and strings and maybe leave a tacky residue deeper in the weave.

I tucked my bottom lip between my front teeth

and checked my watch. 9:07. The buffet would be in high gear, the Millwood's guests gathered at the common room table, Marge shuffling between them and the kitchen with her overloaded silver serving trays. She had a little freezer unit down in the basement for extra food storage, and I could probably manage to slip down to it without being spotted. *If* I timed things right and was quiet about it.

I took off my sneakers, stood up, went back downstairs in my stocking feet, and poked my head out over the bottom rail for a look across the foyer into the kitchen. I could see Marge's wide back (and wider rump) moving away from me to the left, and toward the common room. *Perfect*, I thought.

I padded over to the basement door on the opposite side, yanked it open, and scooted through.

Five minutes later I was back upstairs squatting over Gummi Bear, a determined expression on my face, a Ziploc bag stuffed with ice cubes in my hand. For his part, Gummi Bear beamed a cute, cheerful smile up at the table's undersurface; never mind that his tiny arms and legs had been mashed hopelessly out of shape in some kid's mouth. Maybe Gummi Bear was content to stay put there on the rug. Or maybe he was on a concentrated sugar high—I mean, consider his *ingredients*.

It made no difference to me why Gummi Bear was smiling, however.

He had to go.

I lowered the plastic bag of ice on top of him, knowing the cold would harden the gum and make it easy to pick apart with one of my Japanese skewers. It was something I'd figured out when I was about nine years old. Don't ask me how or why. The clean gene works in mysterious ways.

Now all I needed to do was be patient.

Waiting under the table, I settled back on my heels and started to think, just sort of free-associating the way I always do when I'm unoccupied. I thought about sloppy, destructive kids and the irresponsible parents who let them get away with ruining other people's property, and I wondered why hotels and inns didn't want special down payments for children like they did for pets—particularly children with sticky, dirty faces. I guessed that would be a discriminatory practice, but why differentiate between somebody's kids possibly ruining a sofa and somebody else's dog or cat doing the same? Either way, adults needed to be responsible. And as a cleaning professional, I was all too aware of one of life's deepest profundities: Messes are messes, and none are any good.

I looked down at the carpet, pressed the ice bag down with my palm. A couple of minutes had ticked by, and Gummi Bear needed a bit longer to get hard, sick pun kind of intended. It occurred to me that if I owned an inn, I'd try to cater to senior citizens. They were the neatest, most orderly patrons by far. And their animals were always the neatest, well, animals. Look at Old Abe's tuxedo cat, Skiball. She was loud, true. But in a winning way. And besides never having damaged anything, she was impeccable, the perfect self-cleaning pet. I got along with Skiball, I got along with Old Abe, and I guessed I got along with seniors as a group, although there were, of course, exceptions . . .

I sighed now, scratched behind my ear, and let my gaze roam around the hallway, trying to decide what portion of the Slobby Bunch's gratuitous carnage I'd tackle next.

Then I noticed the blemish on the wallpaper outside Mr. Monahan's door. The very expensive flocked Italian wallpaper, that is.

"My God, are those kids *made* out of goop?" I said under my breath, imagining a variation of *Pinocchio* in which Papa Gepetto made candy instead of wooden toys. Whip together eight parts sucrose, one and a half parts gelatin, a smidgeon of FDA-approved food coloring, and voilà—a live-and-sticky little boy or girl, depending on the preferred mold.

I got out from under the table, snatched up my cleaning bag by the strap, drifted numbly over to Old Abe's door, and just kind of stared at the ugly mark on the wall. It was a fingerprint, or a smeary partial fingerprint, and looked like dried ice cream to me—maybe with some cherry or strawberry syrup mixed in. A sundae, I decided, absolutely positive that Mr. Monahan couldn't have been to blame. No one but my demonic little adversaries could've left behind that schmutz.

I thought for a moment, then dropped my cleaning kit heavily at my feet and bent to rummage inside it for my water bottle and a sponge. If dabbing with plain H_2O didn't get the blotch off the wallpaper, my fallback would be trying the cleaning dough I'd picked up at a local hardware store. The stuff was kind of hard right out of the container, but when you kneaded it in your hand it became pliable enough to roll up and use like a soft pencil eraser. Except that it worked *better* than an eraser, because you could fold the dough over when its surface got too soiled and start again with a clean surface.

But I'd gotten way ahead of myself. The water-and-sponge method seemed to be working fine. Probably, *thankfully*, the smudge was pretty fresh and hadn't had time to set.

A short while later I'd managed to dab or blot every last bit of it from the wallpaper. Sighing with relief, I put away the water and sponge, started turning back down the hall to check the progress of the Gummi-Beared rug—

And then all at once thought I heard the thin, mewling cry of a cat from inside Old Abe's room.

I stopped, facing the door. There it was again. Definitely a cat. Definitely *Skiball*. While I was no feline expert, her excited carrying-on gave me the clear sense that she was in distress. There was something about the muffled faintness of her cries that made me wonder if she'd gotten trapped, maybe in a closet or the bathroom.

My brow crinkled. Figuring I should investigate, I reached for the doorknob, entered the room—if you've ever been to a New England inn, you know they hardly ever bother with locks—and realized that my guess was dead on. There was a clothes closet to my immediate left, and I could tell at once that Skiball was inside it, helplessly trying to tunnel her way to freedom with her little white declawed paws.

Skiball McQueen, I thought.

I hurried over to the closet, pulled it open, and lifted the cat out to comfort her.

But Skiball, who normally feasts on attention, wanted no part of me.

Instead she sprang from my arms, darted around the enormous four-poster in the middle of the room, and started mewling and wailing all over again.

Mystified, I stepped around to the far side of the bed and glanced down to where she'd parked herself.

Then I screamed in horror.

Old Abe was lying there at my feet. Lying sprawled on his back with his eyes open, his neck bent at an impossible angle, and blood soaking into the carpet from a terrible gash on his head.

Screaming louder—so loud I thought it would rip my vocal cords to shreds—I grabbed Skiball up again, tucked her against my side, and forced my feet to move underneath me, rushing out into the hall even as I heard footsteps hurrying upstairs, heard voices shouting to ask what was wrong, what in the world was *going on—*

One of the last things I remember before I fainted was suddenly picturing the fingerprint on the wallpaper outside the door. The print I'd carefully dabbed out of existence.

I had the nasty feeling I'd just done away with important evidence to a crime and would live to regret it. And how.

Sky, you fussy fool! I thought hysterically.

And that was when the world went bye-bye.

Chapter 2

"So you're sure that fingerprint was *all* you scrubbed away?" Chief Vega said.

From his accusatory tone, you'd have thought I destroyed the evidence on purpose.

"Dabbed," I said. "If I'd scrubbed it, the paper would have peeled right off the wall."

Vega looked at me. I wasn't trying to sound sarcastic. I just wanted to be accurate and describe things the way they had happened, for Old Abe's sake.

"Okay," he said. "*Dabbed.*"

It was the morning after I'd found Abe's body, and I was sitting across a desk from Vega in the town police station on Main Street, around the corner from the Fog Bell Inn, where I rented a room from Chloe Edwards, who I may have mentioned is my best friend and positive-vibe energizer. Every day at nine o'clock sharp we'd get together for coffee, and though I'd raced out for my appointment with the chief at eight for what he'd described as a "ten-minute conversation to tie up some loose ends" from my previous statement, we'd already gone way past that supposed ten minutes, which put me in danger of missing Chloe.

She would, of course, understand, given the circumstances. But I was anxious to talk with her and knew she'd have to whisk off somewhere or other pretty soon. This is because she was always whisking off somewhere.

I sat waiting for more questions. Until that horrible weekend I'd never spoken to Chief Vega besides maybe to say hello on the street, and I wasn't quite sure what to make of him—which put me in a class of my own. Everyone else in town seemed to have a well-formed opinion of our new top cop. In fact, if the residents of Pigeon Cove had been polled about it, I have no doubt the results would have split sharply along gender lines. Men tended to resent Alejandro Vega, while women swooned over him.

These were equal but opposite reactions to the same set of qualities, the foremost being that Chief Vega was one handsome hombre. He was also the first police chief ever who wasn't well past middle age and descended from the Anglo-Saxon shipbuilders that settled the town in the 1600s. For the males of Pigeon Cove, Vega's Boston origins made him an unfamiliar target of suspicion and, as a youthful authority figure, a vague threat to their masculinity. To females his background made him especially appealing—and his dark good looks and snugly fitting uniform didn't damage his cause any either. As Chloe had once put it, he was what Antonio Banderas might be if he could occasionally toss aside his carb counter and wolf down a hamburger, fries, and a Coke. Not that Chloe had inside knowledge of Antonio's dietary habits, but I got what she meant. Somehow I couldn't picture him eating a juicy red-meat burger for lunch. He seemed more the Giga-Moto oysters with ginger-sherry mignonette type.

At any rate, the last thing on my mind that morning was Vega's stud factor relative to the movie stars. I'd leave it to someone else to imagine him wearing nothing except a strategically placed badge. I just wanted to help his police work however I could and then rush over to see Chloe before she left on her latest escapade, whatever it might be.

"I found that Gummi Bear on the rug and went to get a bag of ice," I told him now.

"So you could scrape . . . um, remove it."

"Harden it up, yes. My next step would have been to pick it off very carefully with a bamboo skewer."

Chief Vega looked enthralled by the unsolicited cleaning hint—if you could call a blank stare "enthralled." I waited for him to let out a sigh, but he didn't.

Instead he glanced at the notes he'd scribbled on his pad while taking my statement at Marge's. At the time I was a babbling wreck on the living room sofa, which was why Vega had asked to re-interview me the very next day. Or that's what I'd supposed. Given my dazed state of mind after finding Old Abe, even *I* didn't trust anything I might have told him.

"When you went down to the freezer," he said, "did you notice anything out of the ordinary?"

I shook my head no.

"You're positive?" he said. "Think back. Nothing in the hall outside Mr. Monahan's room. Or on the stairs. Or down in that foyer near the door . . ."

"No," I said, and hesitated a little. "There's no foyer near the door."

"The entry hall, then—"

"There's no entry hall either."

Vega gave me one of his irritated looks again. I guess he figured I was picking verbal nits, but I don't like being careless with words. For me it's important to be precise with them. And it should be, considering I write for a minuscule fraction of my very modest living.

"The area, space, whatever." He held back a sigh. "Inside the main door—"

"Is the foyer," I said, and abruptly understood the reason for his confusion. "I took the back stairs."

Vega reviewed his notes, tugged his ear.

"Back stairs?" he said.

"The captain's stairs," I said. "That's what they're called, I have no idea why. And please don't give me another dirty look or scold me again, because I'm trying to cooperate and I can really do without that sort of thing right now."

Vega's eyes rose from the pad to my face.

"What do you mean?" he said.

"How about we start with the 'dirty look' part and take it from there?" I said, and made a puss to illustrate.

He hesitated. "If I've been doing that—"

"You have. And worse."

Vega paused, shook his head, rubbed the back of his neck.

"It's been a long twenty-four hours, Ms. Taylor," he said.

"Tell me about it," I said.

Vega finally released the sigh he'd been holding in.

"Okay," he said. "No more of those looks."

I decided I could live with accepting that as an apology.

"Appreciate it," I said. "And, yes, I took the back stairs so Marge wouldn't see me." I paused a second as Vega jotted something on his pad, and then told him about the chewed candy stuck to Marge's fancy Persian rug. "She would've been sick to her stomach if she'd found out about the Gummi Bear. I was hoping I could sneak some ice up and get it off before she did."

We were both quiet.

"About the stairs," Vega said. "The captain's stairs, I mean. Don't they lead straight down to a back door?"

I nodded.

"*Wind* down is more like it," I said, which was

putting it mildly. The staircase was treacherously narrow and curving, and I always figured that one wrong step would lead to a serious tumble.

"Get to the bottom, open the door, and you're in the backyard, right?" Vega said.

I nodded a second time.

"And there's the stockade fence around the yard and a swing gate?"

"Yes."

"That opens onto Congress Street . . ."

"Yes."

"And do you remember noticing whether it— I'm talking about the back door now—might've been ajar? As if, say, someone had run down those stairs in a hurry."

I shook my head.

"It isn't as if I looked," I said. "I doubt it would've stayed open, though."

He glanced up from his pad.

"Why's that?"

"There are two doors. The inner one and the outer screen door. And since it was a beautiful day, the inner door was open to let in the breeze. But the screen door has a spring."

"Spring?"

"A spring closer." I made a pushing gesture. "You know. Open the door, the closer makes it swing shut nice and tight."

Vega considered that.

"Those things do loosen up after a while," he said, thinking aloud. "Get rusty—"

I shook my head again.

"Marge's is brand-new," I said. "I installed it myself."

Vega's surprised expression was typical of what I get whenever I mention my knack for home repairs to guys who don't know me. It comes with being a woman who's five five and weighs 120 pounds.

"I did it just last month," I told him before he could ask. "We knew Mr. Monahan was coming for his regular Memorial Day visit—"

I suddenly choked up, feeling a rush of sorrow at the awareness that those stays were now a thing of the past. Still, clogged throat aside, I was holding up okay. For months after my husband's death, I would cry at the slightest sad thought. In all honesty, it was even worse than that; I can recall instances when I'd be set off for no apparent reason. But after a while I'd managed to get the waterworks under control, helped along by deep-breathing exercises from an instructional DVD my parents sent me—it was called *Dr. Jasper Silk's Tantric Keys to Emotional Balance*, and I must admit the results had been a total surprise. Jasper Silk wasn't a medical doctor but had a Ph.D. in philosophy. He was also an herbalist, a homeopathist, and a new paradigm healer, whatever that last was supposed to mean. For two ex–flower children like Mom and Dad, who were devoted listeners of Silk's public radio talk show, his emphasis on alternative wellness methods qualified him as the perfect pop guru. For me it had smelled suspiciously of quack, and that opinion hadn't totally changed. I couldn't argue with what worked, though. And the breathing exercises did do the trick.

"We knew Abe had booked his room, and the old pneumatic closer was shot and needed to be replaced before he arrived," I resumed with a practiced Silkian inhalation, proud I hadn't gotten all weak and tearful in front of Vega.

He waited, his pen hovering above his pad.

"There a particular reason?" he said.

I nodded. "Marge and Chloe . . . that's my friend Chloe Edwards . . . are the only innkeepers in town who are pet-friendly bookers. And Marge, who's got two Welsh corgis and a Pekingese of her own, was having a problem with them getting out into the backyard through that screen door."

"Because it wasn't latching shut properly," he said.

"Right. They're very strong dogs, especially the corgis," I said. "So when Abe confirmed his reservation, we figured we'd better get it fixed, since he always brings along . . . that is, always brought his—"

I stopped talking and gaped at Vega.

"Oh, no!" I said. "Skiball!"

"What?"

"Skiball!"

Vega looked at me as if he thought I'd gone into Zoloft withdrawal.

He rose slightly from his chair, motioned toward the watercooler. "Ms. Taylor, I'd better get you a drink—"

"Mr. Monahan's cat!" I explained, and saw dawning comprehension on his features. "He always drove up to Marge's with his cat, and she was stuck in his closet, and I got her out, and was carrying her under my arm when—" I stopped again. "Do you know what happened to Skiball after I fainted?"

Vega had sat back down, nodding. He seemed relieved to see I hadn't gone bonkers.

"The cat's unharmed," he said. "We took it to Boston."

"Boston?"

"For examination."

I looked at him.

"A *forensic* exam," Vega clarified.

I waited for him to go on.

"Animals at crime scenes may collect hairs, clothing fibers, skin, other trace evidence on their bodies that would help identify the perpetrator," he said. "Mr. Monahan's cat had blood on one of her paws . . ."

"Blood?" I said.

"Right," Vega said. "Just a speck—"

"On one of her little white *paws*?"

Vega nodded. His expression said he was glad I hadn't noticed that when I'd rescued her from the closet, and washed it into oblivion like I'd done the wallpaper stain.

"It was barely visible. As I said, a speck. But we don't know if it belongs to the cat, Mr. Monahan, or someone else who may have gained entry to the room." Vega paused. "It—the cat—Skibell, that is—"

"Ski*ball*!"

"Skiball, sorry, won't be harmed," he said. "The forensics people should finish their work this morning, if they haven't done so already. Once they're done, she'll be turned over to a city shelter."

I stared at him.

"A *what*?"

"A shelter for homeless and abandoned animals," he said. "Abe Monahan has no known relatives to claim it. Or none we can locate anyway. And that actually leads me to another question—"

"Poor Skiball," I interrupted.

Vega offered a smile that I guessed was meant to reassure me.

"It's the best thing for the cat," he said.

"Wonderful," I said.

"A humane solution," he said, still smiling.

"Wonderful *and* humane," I said.

"For the cat," he repeated.

We sat and looked at each other. I imagined Skiball in one of those institutional wire kennels at the shelter. Imagined poor, impeccable Skiball having to use shredded newspapers instead of litter when she did her business—and in the same cage where they'd put her food dish. Then I took another slow Silkian breath, holding it to balance my *prana* and thereby manage my formerly push-button emotions.

After about ten or fifteen seconds of that, I started bawling like a fool.

Chapter 3

There are at least three long-standing ordinances in Pigeon Cove that restrict the exterior color of homes in its historic districts. I think about ninety-nine percent of our dwellings fall into that category, with the rest spaced around its southern and western outskirts, where you'll also find the dump, the public sewage facility, a defunct seafood-processing plant, and some storage units run by a reclusive and legendarily grumpy guy named Rollie Evers. Old Abe had rented one of them for years, keeping it stocked with cartons and other packing materials that he used to prepare his book sale finds for shipment to his place in Florida.

The closer you are to those unattractive chunks of real estate, the lower your property tax and the less your residential paint palette is liable to concern the town council. Arguably, a person with nonconformist tendencies would prefer to be ignored by that bunch of snoots—something I should know as the daughter of two tie-dyed oddballs who've got a huge peace sign painted on the side of their house. But I've learned from people at the newspaper that living on the fringes can stink when your roads and sidewalks need improvement. Neighborhood preservation rules work both ways.

Main Street, as its name suggests, runs through the very heart of historic Pigeon Cove. The B&Bs, gift shops, and art galleries along that vital artery—I promise not to stretch the anatomical metaphor here much further—are the lifeblood nourishing our little hamlet's economy and must strictly meet its color-coded traditions and standards. That generally requires clapboard white for Colonial and Victorian buildings, although light, reserved beige is considered acceptable. Sprinkled into the mix are some prim blue-gray Federals and Queen Annes, and one or two stately redbrick Georgians. Also covered by the ordinances are the quaint little saltboxes tucked away in Pigeon Cove's lanes, waterfront walks, and pocket beaches. As the architectural stuff that New England picture postcards are made of, these can pass with weathered brown shingle if they're well maintained.

All that said, Chloe Edwards's Fog Bell Inn stands prominently pink in the middle of Main Street. Not shocking pink, mind you, but a sort of elegant dusty rose. I don't quite know how Chloe got around the color codes. I do know that her abundant personal charm is a factor. Chloe's boundless zest isn't just contagious, it's addictive.

Put simply, she *shines*. Five minutes of exposure to her is a definite pick-me-up. Ten can turn a lousy day around. Fifteen minutes and she'll not only make you feel the world's at your fingertips, but have you wanting to do something nice for her in return—and she realizes it.

Chloe can be a shrewd dispenser of her generosity, an expert at playing the system to her advantage while showing a genuine community consciousness. She does volunteer work for all kinds of local causes, and it never hurts that some of them are of sincere concern not only to her but to the Cove's most influential people as well. Town councilmen welcome her voting drives; the Cape Ann orchestra owes her a huge debt for the black-tie benefit dinners she throws at Christmastime; the library can count on raking in thousands of dollars yearly from her Fourth of July weekend "bake 'n' book" sales. Chloe even managed to endear herself to the fishermen—who usually don't take to anybody not wearing waders—after she sweet-talked the Cove's deep-pockets types into establishing a college scholarship fund for their kids.

I've already said I draw a charge off Chloe's vitality and am convinced the rest of the town does the same—for me, she's the heart and soul of Pigeon Cove. I literally don't know where I'd be without her, but more on that in a while. Right now I want to get back to the morning after I found Old Abe's body.

As I raced over to the Fog Bell from the police

station, I was hoping I hadn't missed Chloe altogether and regretting I'd told her not to wait if I was late. But another of my best friend's qualities is her unfailing punctuality, and I hadn't wanted to get in its way. Chloe holds her time at a premium. With all the appointments crammed into her schedule, she barely has a choice.

And so I turned into her yard at a full trot and hustled up the gravel path wiggling through its English garden. Chloe's husband, Oscar, is a retired orchestra musician, and I could hear him blowing something classical on his clarinet through an open downstairs window. Oscar never leaves the house without a fight. Or answers the door without one. Or the telephone for that matter. Basically, Oscar doesn't do anything except toot away in the den until Chloe yanks his instrument from his hands because he's driving her guests crazy. You'd think he'd also be driving them to take their business elsewhere, but it isn't the case. Maybe it's because the sounds he makes are generally agreeable; he's a really accomplished tooter. And Oscar can be pretty charming in his own cranky way. Still, though, visitors at a B&B generally rank peace and quiet high among their preferences, and it would be nice if there could be a little around the house now and then.

I mention this only to explain why Chloe always keeps her front door unlocked during the day. When she's home it's difficult to hear the bell through Oscar's racket. When she's out, Oscar won't bother getting off his chair to answer—if he miraculously hears its chime. Guests either have to let themselves in or risk waiting indefinitely for Chloe to show up at the entrance.

Making my way to the front porch, I passed a crowd of hedges and flower boxes that had been nudged into early bloom by our unusually warm and rainy spring weather. Daisies and hollyhocks swarmed the path; morning glories clambered over trellises; cosmos spilled wildly over the porch railing. Off to the right of the porch, I could see the herb patch that was one of my minor personal touches to the yard. Chloe had always grown her own herbs and vegetables, but she'd kept them tucked away in the back garden till I offered to move them in close to the front porch, informing her that basil and rosemary repelled mosquitoes and other little winged thingies she didn't want flying through her windows. When the herbs started to attract Japanese beetles, which were *giant* winged thingies that liked munching on herbs and vegetables, I put a border of yellow and orange marigolds around the herb patch to get rid of them. Japanese beetles tend to avoid marigolds. I'm not sure why, and don't especially care. I tend to avoid Japanese beetles irrespective of their likes and dislikes.

At the bottom of the porch steps, I paused to break a spike of lavender from the clump that was another of my additions to Chloe's yard. Rubbing it between my thumb and forefinger, I kind of patted the fragrance onto my neck. Perfume *au naturel*.

Then it was up to the Fog Bell's door.

Once inside, you pass through a foyer into an inviting parlor with large bay windows and a bunch of comfortable chairs arranged around an antique German woodstove. Just beyond that a formal dining room opens into the kitchen.

That was where I found Chloe, dancing near the sink with her back to me and singing in the highest of high sopranos over the music from Oscar's den. I emphasize the word "over," which is very different from singing along. Oscar was practicing a Mozart piece, and I don't think Amadeus ever mentioned hemi-powered drones in his lyrics, or invited anybody to wrap his or her legs around his velvet rims.

"Tramps like us, baby, we were born to run!" Chloe let out as I watched, swinging her hips, rolling her shoulders, and doing some kind of weird helicopter move with her arms.

With that she lunged for the counter and jabbed a button on the electric blender on top of it.

It started to whir. Or maybe I should say it droned like a hemi. Chloe has what you'd call a muscle blender.

I couldn't resist a smile. Though I knew I'd have to rush right out of the place, it was a relief to find Chloe at home. Also, I recognized the song trilling from her lips. The refined, decorous, and mannerly Chloe Edwards—who'd been vaguely sixtyish when I met her ten years back, and still seemed vaguely sixtyish, and would no doubt be vaguely sixtyish till the sun went nova and burned everything on Earth to cinders, like the Discovery Channel keeps reminding us will happen—was getting down with a Springsteen number.

The frothy head of soapsuds I noticed in the blender was another kick.

As I stood there in the entrance, Chloe spun around on the balls of her feet, still gyrating to some inner accompaniment. I wasn't sure if she'd heard me, or executed some sort of funky dance move that just happened to coincide with my appearance.

"Fill your blender halfway with warm water and a drop of dishwashing liquid," she belted out with a hip-shaking flourish. She'd matched the words to the melody and rhythm of Bruce's signature anthem—and done a good job. "Turn on the blender, and any goop stuck to the bottom of the blades will whip loose!"

For those who care, that last line fell in rhythmically with the Boss singing about the highway being jammed with broken heroes, unpleasant imagery that suggests playing with hemis can do grave damage to the human body.

"Hell-ooo-ooo!" Chloe chirped now. "Have you seen what I'm doing?"

I took that to mean what she was doing besides her dance routine. Which I had. It gratified me, since I'd given her the blender-cleaning tip only days before.

"Don't forget to rinse," I said, nodding with approval.

"Yes!" she said amid the onslaught of wood-wind music and blender noises around us. "Thoroughly! With cold water!"

Chloe didn't always speak in singsong exclamations. But she knew how miserable my last twenty-four hours had been, and I suspected her overflowing cheeriness was a deliberate attempt to lift my spirits.

"Chloe, listen," I said, a little breathless after hurrying from the police station. "I just came from talking to Chief Vega—"

"Wait a moment, dear! Tell me once we sit down!"

She turned off the foaming blender, snatched my wrist, and guided me toward her sunny little breakfast nook table.

"Chloe, I can't stay," I said. Out of the corner of my eye, I saw guiltily that she'd set the table with a thermal coffeepot, cups, dishes, and a serving tray heaped with muffins and scones. "I've got to drive down to Boston."

"Boston?" she said. "Now?"

I was nodding. "Right now."

From the look Chloe gave me, you would have thought I'd told her I was heading off to down-town Jallalabad for a women's rights protest. That didn't surprise me. People from Cape Ann tend to be phobic about leaving their respective hamlets. It's as if they're afraid you tumble into another dimension after crossing the Annisquam Bridge.

"You aren't in any trouble, are you?" Chloe asked. She was born in a village called Tottenham outside London, and her faint British accent had begun to surface. It always does when she's upset.

"No, Chloe, I'm okay."

"You're sure there wasn't some misunderstanding with Chief Vega? Your eyes are all red."

I didn't want to tell her I'd broken down in tears at the police station. She was agitated enough without having to hear it.

"It's my new contact lenses," I lied.

"You told me that you loved the new contacts."

"I'd love them more if they didn't feel like slices of cayenne pepper," I said. "Besides, what kind of trouble would I be in?"

Chloe stared at me. I stared back at her. Then it struck me.

Have I mentioned that Chloe has a wild imagination fueled by dual addictions to mystery novels and Court TV?

"Chloe," I said, incredulous. "You don't think . . ."

"Oh, no! Of course I don't!"

"You do! I *never* would've done anything to hurt Mr.—"

"Surely, you wouldn't, dear. But accidents will happen. And you *were* asked to the police station for questioning." She hesitated. "Should you ever have to go on the lam, if that's the term, I would hope you'd feel free to ask me for, ah, some flight money."

"Chloe, this is nuts. Abe was my *friend*."

"I know he was. Still, lawmen are fallible and might get the wrong idea. Even the best of friends can have a falling-out. Take Donald Trump and Martha Stewart, can you believe those two? And then there's Bill Drecksel. He and Abe Monahan were close. Before Mr. Monahan was killed, of course."

I stood there trying to process that. Bill Drecksel owned a diner, known for its drecky, watered-down coffee, on the Gull Wing, a curving point of land that flares into the harbor and bristles with restaurants, shops, and fishing wharves.

"Hang on," I said. "What about Bill and Mr. Monahan? Did something happen between them?"

Chloe nodded.

"I thought you knew. Old Abe was over at Bill's place early in the morning yesterday. Again, before he was killed."

"Chloe, no offense. But it's kind of *understood* this would be when Abe was alive."

"Yes, sorry. I suppose it is," she said. "Anyway, they got into quite a shouting match. Jessie Barton overheard them when she was getting up a display in her store window."

I looked at her, still trying to figure things out. Jessie Barton owned a clothing shop next door to the diner. Along with Chloe, she was also a founding member of the Do-Re-Mis, an a cappella group that was one of three competing female vocal ensembles on Cape Ann—the others being the La-dee-da Girls and the stodgily venerable forerunner of them all, Classical Glee.

"When did Jessie tell you about them having an argument?" I said after a few seconds.

"Last night," Chloe said. "She's been up to her ears finishing the song list for our performance tomorrow. That's what she mainly phoned to discuss. And why I was practicing the Boss when you came in."

"Has Jessie spoken to the police yet?" I said.

"About the song list?"

"About the argument, Chloe," I said.

Chloe looked thoughtful for a moment.

"Jessie's very defensive when it comes to Bill, have you noticed? Just ask her about his coffee, and she'll tell you she *loves* it, which I believe makes her the only person in town who drinks it. Well, aside from tourists who don't know any better."

Chloe, as you can see, occasionally seems to have problems staying on track. But that's a misperception. If you're patient, and learn to follow along with her way of thinking, you'll usually wind up headed in the right direction—and maybe even pick up an insight or two. The trick is knowing when to help her make herself clear.

"You're telling me Jessie didn't call the police," I said.

Chloe nodded.

"I suggested that to her, but she seems reluctant," she said. "I think she's afraid Bill's threats might be blown out of proportion."

"Bill *threatened* Abe?"

"Well, that's the question right there," Chloe said. "Jessie did say that when we started out our conversation. But when I asked her what sort of threats she meant, she turned around and insisted they weren't really threats. She says Bill likes to holler, but that's as far as it ever goes."

"Did she tell you what he was hollering?" I said.

Chloe shook her head.

"I wondered about that too. She told me she wasn't interested in listening in on them and couldn't remember very much of what she did hear."

If that was what she claimed, I didn't buy it. Jessie used my cleaning service on a regular basis, and I'd gotten to like her well enough. But while she was generally decent, she did have something of an opportunistic streak and always kept her ears tuned to the local gossip band for fresh intelligence. A quarrel she found worth mentioning was one she'd have paid close attention to.

I stood there trying to digest everything I'd heard, and realized it had made me more mystified than ever.

"I still can't imagine why anybody would lose their temper with Abe," I said, summing up my thoughts.

"Nor can I, dear," Chloe said. "But it looks as

if someone did in a big way, doesn't it?" She paused, shrugged. "You know, I feel almost indecent singing so soon after a tragedy. But there's a rehearsal in an hour. We're branching out from choral music, throwing some rock 'n' roll into the mix, and I need to get ready." Chloe raised her hands over her head, snapped her fingers like a mariachi dancer, and did something slinky with her waist. "The show must go on."

I was quiet for a minute. Life on Cape Ann is a constant series of adjustments to peculiarity.

"Chloe," I said, "Jessie better call Chief Vega. I mean, toot sweet. Before I left his office, he asked whether Abe might've been having problems with anyone. In town, outside town, whatever. But I couldn't think of a single person who didn't like Abe. Never mind that I was blubbering too hard to answer."

Chloe gave me a sharp look, and I realized I'd slipped up.

"So you *were* crying at the station!" she said. "I knew you were in trouble. What sort of awful bum rap are they trying to lay on you, dear?"

I shook my head, thinking Chloe really did need to be weaned off those crime stories. For her own good.

"Chloe, I'm okay," I said, and then told her about Skiball being taken to the shelter. "That's why I've got to shoot down to Boston."

"If you wait till later, I could ride down with you when my rehearsal's finished. Keep you company—"

"I *can't* wait," I said. "They don't have a no-kill policy."

Chloe looked at me. "Surely they wouldn't . . . you know . . . do anything *final* to her in so short a time."

"I'd hope not, Chloe. But they wouldn't make any firm guarantees when I phoned from Vega's office. These places are overcrowded and understaffed and I can't risk a screwup." I paused. "Besides, I want to head over to the newspaper this afternoon."

Chloe kept looking at me. Tall, slim, and strikingly attractive in her ageless way, she was wearing a cotton boatneck pullover with a pastel flower print, black capri pants, and low-heeled ballet slippers. Her chin-length ash-blond hair was brushed back from her face, and she'd put on a neutral shade of lipstick and simple gold hoop earrings that gave her a certain understated stylishness.

"I appreciate your offer, Chloe," I said after a second. "But I'll be there and back again in a couple of hours."

Chloe's features were showing a bit less worry than before.

"All right," she said finally. "But at least let me wrap a muffin or two for your trip."

"That'd be super, Chloe."

"And you'll phone on my cell if you have any problems?"

"Promise you'll try to persuade Jessie to contact Chief Vega and you've got a deal," I said.

Chloe gave me her word that she'd do her best, and went to wrap the muffins. As she brought them over in a small brown bag, I suddenly remembered the lavender sprig in my hand.

"Would you mind dropping this in that basket I've got in the kitchen?" I said, holding it out. "The one with all the others I picked for my fresh batch of oil?"

Chloe took it even as she gave me the bag.

"Just in the nick of time," she said. "I've used up my supply."

"Same here," I said. "When I cleaned the Thompson house the other day, I put the last few drops in a new vacuum cleaner bag, figuring the heat from the motor would release the scent."

"And it worked?" she said.

I nodded.

"The more I vacuumed, the flowerier the room started smelling," I said, and then quickly explained how that masterstroke led me to come up with another of my aromatic bug deterrents. I'd remembered reading somewhere or other that moths stay away from lavender, which gave me the idea to vacuum the Thompsons' clothes closets—they have a couple of enormous walk-ins—using the scented bag. "Give it a try, Chloe. Keeps your clothes fragrant and the moths out."

Her marveling smile confirmed that she felt better than she had a minute ago. I did too, thanks to the Chloe Force.

"Lavender oil on a vacuum cleaner bag," she

said, and shook her head. "How in the world do you think of these things?"

I shrugged. In the background, Oscar's clarinet playing had reached a tunefully maddening peak.

"They say everybody's got an inborn talent," I said. "Guess that's mine."

Chapter 4

"Yii-ii-eee," Skiball said.

I kept my hands on the steering wheel and glanced over at the cardboard pet carrier beside me. It was rocking back and forth as Skiball smushed her face against the vent holes and tried to paw her way out.

"Take it easy," I said. "You'll be a free cat in no time."

That didn't placate her. The carrier kept rocking on the passenger seat.

"Rroooooeoo!" she protested.

I stayed quiet, unable to think of an answer.

We were headed back to Pigeon Cove from the animal shelter, driving north on Route 128 past the shopping mall in Peabody, where the old Filene's department store had been converted to a Macy's, and the space previously occupied by Macy's across the mall was on its way to becoming a Nordstrom, a semi-upscale retailer based somewhere out in the Pacific Northwest—Seattle,

I think, but don't hold me to it. An article in the *Boston Globe* had said the out-of-town chain store would be a "dashing anchor" for the mall, and then had gone on to tell about the hundreds of layoffs that would result from the shuffling of retailers. Meanwhile, the mayor of Peabody had foamed at the mouth about the whole thing being terrific for the area over the long haul. The mayor had been in federal banking and politics his whole life, which just might have influenced his point of view. Whether it did or didn't, I was sure he had a huge golden parachute and didn't have to worry about paying his utility bills or his kids' college tuition if he got voted out of office because of massive unemployment in the short haul.

As I left the mall in my rearview, I was thinking it would have been nice if the *Globe* article had paid more attention to the downside of the mergers and buyouts. For me, the big story was that a lot of working-class families in and around Peabody were about to face years of financial struggle as the local economy was realigned. But what can you expect from a newspaper that owns a chunk of the Boston Red Sox? As a die-hard Yankee fan—Paul had been a season ticket holder, and we'd gone to countless games at the Stadium together—I was hoping the *Globe* would pull a move similar to Filene's and Macy's and change into the *New York Daily News* overnight. Then I could spend my idle moments combing the sports section for shots of Derek Jeter in full, breathtaking extension. In the meantime, I'd be stuck with regular doses of big-butted Red Sox players who resembled unscrubbed russet potatoes—although I will agree that not *all* Sox players are total eyesores. Every so often, I'll see one with potential to be a decent-looking guy under all the dirt, grime, and clumps of peroxide-splattered cornrows. But my preference in men, as with all other aspects of life, is for crisp and clean over ragged and raunchy.

Anyway, I was nearing the first Gloucester roundabout when somebody in the next lane over cut me off for no apparent reason. The jarringly short stop as I was forced to slam on my brakes didn't bother me—a single psycho-driver encounter per ten miles was about average for Route 128, and since I'd been on it for almost twice that distance, I figured I was ahead of the game. Plus my SUV handles short stops very well.

Skiball wasn't as confident and let out another loud protestation in her kitty carrier. Overall, she'd been consistent about her dislike for motor travel, with Greater Boston–area traffic making her especially anxious.

"Aaaaaa!" she said.

I sighed. I'd known Skiball had a large cat vocabulary ever since Old Abe introduced us. What I hadn't realized was that her gabbing was pretty much incessant—and matched by a manic inability to remain still for any length of time. She'd been quiet for five minutes max during our ride, and that was only because she'd fallen asleep with exhaustion from trying to paw her way through the sides of the carrier. After a bump on the road got her going again, she hadn't relented. Twice she became frantic and tipped the carrier over the edge of the seat, screaming with panic as she tumbled head-over-tail inside it like a fuzzy sock in a clothes dryer. Each time I had to wait for another stop in traffic before I could reach over and set her back where she belonged.

When I imagined how she must have acted during her long drives from Florida, I had to wonder at Old Abe's patience. Of course, he'd always said Skiball's tenaciousness was the very trait that got her through his front door.

As Abe told it, he'd found her near his house in Florida while out on his regular morning stroll. He'd lived in one of those gated communities in the southwestern part of the state, and would walk about a mile every day, sometimes heading toward an area that the bulldozers hadn't yet razed for new homes. Abe enjoyed watching for reptiles and exotic birds, and had once found a tortoise in the middle of the blacktop, picked it up, and set it in the roadside brush so it would be safe from passing cars. The next morning he decided to take the same route and, coming up to where he'd left the tortoise, observed some movement on the road ahead. The palms were throwing heavy shadows across the blacktop, playing tricks with his vision, and he'd thought at first that it was the same slowpoke tortoise making its way across the road again. But then he noticed it was heading toward him faster than any tortoise could move, and heard the noise it was making and realized it was a little cat. Though declawed, she wasn't wearing a collar and looked thinner than she probably should have been. She also seemed desperate for companionship, following Abe all the way home and carrying on the entire way there.

Dropping her off in his lanai, Abe drove out to the supermarket and bought several cans of cat food, which she gobbled up in a flash. But then he got the idea that she might have an owner who was looking for her. Cats, after all, can wander pretty far from home once they're out the door.

Abe hadn't wanted to be an inadvertent cat thief. He also hadn't wanted the responsibility of owning a pet. So he drove Skiball back to where he'd found her—putting up with some seriously annoying antics, I bet—and left her in the foliage the same as he'd done with the tortoise. Two hours later, he returned to check on whether she'd hung around waiting for him. When he didn't see her, he told himself that she must have gone home and started driving away again. But then he pulled over on an impulse, got out of his car, and walked to the exact spot where he'd put her down. Something inside him had told him to make absolutely sure she wasn't there.

That was when Abe started calling her Skiball. He never knew why the name popped into his head—right up to that point she'd just been "little kitty" to him. But he called her a single time, and after a couple of seconds heard her rustling and meowing somewhere in the grass. And then she shot out of it and jumped into his arms, wrapping her cotton-soft forelegs around his neck.

"She hugged me like a baby girl who found her papa!" Abe had recalled.

Afterward, he'd put flyers up around the neighborhood that said he'd found a lost cat and gave his phone number in case Skiball's owner wanted to claim her, but no one ever responded. And for some reason or other, he hadn't believed anybody would. Skiball was his. Or maybe I should say Abe was hers. If you've ever lived with a cat, you'll know what I mean.

My personal education really started the day I drove her back from Boston.

Not that I could bring Skiball right home after signing her out of the shelter. First, I needed to head over to the *Cape Ann Anchor* and get some work done on my weekly column. I was inching up to my filing deadline and hadn't thought about it at all in the last twenty-four hours. While I had good reason, and knew my editor wouldn't fault me for turning in my piece late under the circumstances, I figured it was a good idea to focus on something constructive instead of dwelling morbidly on what had happened to Old Abe.

The *Anchor*'s headquarters consist of a plain two-story office building outside Gloucester about half a mile past the traffic circle. Swinging off Route 128, I took the road that leads to the industrial park, drove on past it, and made a quick right into the *Anchor*'s parking lot, where I saw maybe three or four cars nosed in front of the entrance.

I pulled in alongside them, unstrapped myself, and started reaching for the pet carrier's handle.

It was then that I noticed a piece of a muffin on the carpet beneath the dash, about an inch off the rubber floor mat.

"Yii-ii-ee," I said in flawless Skiball-ese.

I was thinking that of the two muffins Chloe had given me for the drive to Boston—one a blueberry, the other a chocolate-chocolate chip—I'd gulped down everything but a portion of the chocolate-chocolate chip. Probably it had fallen from the tray between the driver's seat and the passenger seat when I stuck out a hand to steady the pet carrier. The carrier must have landed on top of it when Skiball went overboard, mashing it into the carpet.

All this came to me in a flash. *Sky Taylor's my name, accidental stain removal is my game.* Now I had to move to the damage-control phase. While I didn't have time to clean it, I was not about to have a permanent chocolate eyesore on my carpet.

I picked up the chunk of muffin, took a plastic trash bag out of the glove box, and dumped it inside. Predictably, it left a cocoa brown spot behind on the light gray rug—not a good visual. Moving fast, I backed out my door, zipped around to the hatch, raised it, and got out the six-ounce bottle of club soda that's a staple of my bag of tricks, grabbing a clean rag while I was at it.

Returning to the scene of the stain, I poured a generous amount of club soda onto it, then soaked the rag with more of the fizzy water and covered the spot. The club soda would prevent the stain from setting, the rag would keep the soda from drying, and I would consequently avoid plunging into despair. When I got home, I'd use a cloth lathered with yellow bar soap to blot the rug and lift up the chocolate.

In the meantime, I could forget about it.

"Okay, Skiball, here we go again," I said.

I took hold of the pet carrier's handle, got out of the Toyota, and turned toward the building's glass doors.

Pam DiGallucci sat at the reception desk, appraising us through tinted designer eyeglasses that dwarfed my SUV's windshield in size. A thin, stale-looking blonde in her fifties, she wore enough makeup for an entire Kabuki troupe and had eyebrows that had been waxed and plucked into perfectly defined little arrowheads.

"Eeee-eee!" Skiball said, peering back at her through the carrier's vent holes.

I had to suppress a similar scream. When the Digger caught hold of you there were only two things on her mind. One was digging into your personal affairs. The other was eating your vital organs. Whether these endearing qualities were the cause or effect of three divorces and a runaway husband was an ongoing debate at the *Anchor*.

"Sky, how are you?" she asked.

"All right," I said.

"I'm very glad to hear it. I didn't think we'd see you for a while."

"Well, I'm here."

"Poor girl," she said. "You've had a tough time."

The Digger's red lips parted over her large, bonded white teeth. She was either trying to smile or getting ready to take a bite out of me.

"I suppose it's normal to be sad about your friend, but he had a good run," she said. "He was in his seventies, no?"

I looked at her.

"Around that," I said.

"Listen, when I'm that age, I hope somebody clocks *me* one good on the head before it goes soft."

"Now there's an idea."

"I'm serious, honey." She looked skyward. "If you're listening up there, please make it quick! Better I'm put out of my misery than shipped off to live with my idiot daughter and her husband!"

I nodded past her up the hall. "Got to hurry—"

"No need," the Digger said. "Beverly's taking her mother to the doctor tomorrow and won't be in. So you'll have the office to yourself for an extra day this week."

I hesitated. Bev Snow is the paper's lifestyles and entertainment writer and we share a cubbyhole of an office barely large enough to hold a desk, a computer, and a file cabinet. We'd worked out a schedule that gave me use of it two afternoons a week, with Bev getting dibs the rest of the week. This might sound unfair, but it's actually very decent of her. With Bev being a part-time staffer, and myself a freelance contributor, she's under no obligation to split the tiny space.

"Is Bev's mom okay?" I asked.

"Besides suffering from an incurable need for attention." The Digger leaned forward to eye the pet carrier, her pancake-flat rear end rising off her chair. "What's that in there?" she said.

"A cat," I said.

"A *cat*?"

"Yes."

"How cute."

"Thanks."

"It would make a darling office mascot," the Digger said. Another unholy smile threatened to crack her foundation, which was a sure sign of trouble. Then she sniffled and held a finger under her nose.

"Too bad," she said, "I'm allergic to cats."

Presto.

"Not to worry. She's just visiting," I said.

The Digger put a hand to her chest and coughed.

"Listen to me, I'm already filling with phlegm," she said and made a production of clearing her throat. "Have you heard about that new law in Virginia? Or maybe it's North Carolina. Somewhere down south."

I shook my head. "No, I haven't."

The Digger rolled her eyes behind her enormous lenses.

"You should occasionally try watching the news," she said with a loud snort. "The law bans people from bringing their pets to work. Much as I love animals, exposure to fur and dander is a public health issue."

Skiball shrieked again and I pulled the carrier close against my side.

"Uh-oh," I said.

"My God, what's wrong with it?" the Digger said, and thrust her face up to the carrier for a better look inside. Her allergies must have gone into sudden remission, because she showed no choking symptoms.

"She's having a fit," I said.

"A what?"

"A cat fit," I said. "From cosmetic overkill."

The Digger angled her head at me. Her eyebrows had climbed so perilously close to her hairline I was sure they'd cut a pair of notches into it.

"Better get her away from you before she gags to death," I said, and whipped past the reception desk into the corridor.

Like most small-press newspapers, the *Anchor* runs on a shoestring budget and is an almost entirely self-contained operation. On the ground floor are its editorial, advertising, and production departments. The upper story holds two conference rooms, an employee lounge, and the office suite occupied by our owner and publisher, Boone Stevenson. An easygoing guy who inherited the paper from his late father, Boone seems to have accepted his role as a family obligation rather than come into it with any real journalistic passion— you always get the sense he'd rather be out doing other things, preferably in Speedos and sneakers. Still, Boone has no problem delegating responsibilities to people with the background and inclination to handle them, and he'd picked a young, energetic crew to run the show—a guy named Gregg Connors being the editor in chief. I guess this kind of setup might lead to internal conflicts and power struggles in some cases, but the *Anchor* seems to get along fine. The Digger aside, it's a nice, friendly workplace.

As I headed past its various offices and departments, I wound up wishing everyone would be a bit less effusive with their niceness that particular afternoon. I suppose it was sort of lousy of me— I should have been grateful for their concern. But it was how I felt.

"Sky, you holding together okay?" asked Bob the copy editor from behind a partition.

I answered that I was holding together fine.

"Sky, let me know if there's any way I can help!" said Fiona the ad rep through a doorway.

I told her I would, and that I appreciated the offer.

"Sky, wow, you must be bummed!" Bryan the college intern said from the Webmaster's office.

I admitted I was, but adapted a phrase from one of my mom's favorite songs and reassured him that all bummers must pass.

And so it went, the expressions of support mixed with a question or three about my pet carrier.

I admit it came as a relief when Skiball let out a long, shrill "Eeeeeeaaaaaii!" that scared Pete the pressroom manager into breaking off his condolences. While they were sweet, sincere, and vastly preferable to the Digger's digging, I didn't want to be smothered in sympathy. I'd been through months of that after Paul died—with no one feeling sorrier for me than myself. When I decided to leave New York behind, it was because I was determined to move beyond my grief and get on with living. And in a way that was the same thing that had prompted me to head into the office today. I wasn't trying to stifle my feelings or pretend they didn't exist. I'm not wired for that. But I needed to put one foot in front of the other and push forward.

As I approached my little time-share square of an office, I was all set to shut the door behind me, retreat from the rest of the world, and get down to writing my column.

The only problem was that the door couldn't be shut. Not unless I moved the dozen or so cartons I found stacked in the entryway and propping it wide open.

I frowned. The boxes—the very large boxes—hadn't been there when I'd last been to the office a couple of days before. Nor did they belong there now. Yet here they were, piled chest-high on the carpet, wedging the door back against the wall.

When I tested the weight of the top carton by trying to shift it with both hands, it didn't budge.

"Careful or you'll strain an ab muscle."

It was Bryan again. I looked around as he stepped over to me and instantly I noticed the little studs on the bridge of his nose. I tried not to stare and was semisuccessful, an improvement on my past record of outright gaping at his horrid facial adornments. This made me feel very hip and, what's more, proud of myself. Maybe I'd started getting used to his eyebrow, nostril, lip, and ear piercings, because for a change the new additions didn't seem so much gross-outs as items of curiosity. There were two studs on each side below his tear ducts—a red above a black—and I couldn't for anything imagine how he'd gotten the things plugged through.

"Do you know who put these here?" I said, pulling my eyes off his studs to nod at the boxes.

"Sure," Bryan said. "I did."

"You?"

"Yesterday," he said. "There's all kinds of stuff. Computers, monitors, tons of software."

"For this office?"

"For my office," Bryan said. "We're making improvements to the Web site."

I looked at him. "Your office is way back down the hall."

"Right."

"And can you give me a reason why the boxes aren't in *there*?"

Bryan shrugged.

"Got no place for the new stuff till we get the old stuff out," he said. "All that moving back and forth, I figured we'd need plenty of room in front of our door."

"So you dumped them in front of my door."

"Uh, yeah."

"Even though that means it can't be closed."

Bryan kind of chewed on a silver barbell in the corner of his lip, and I heard it clicking between his teeth.

"Good point," he said. "You want me to stick 'em someplace else?"

I thought about that. Not only was I yearning for some privacy, I'd wanted the door shut so I could let Skiball, who'd been cooped up forever, out of her carrier. But I wasn't sure it was worth the distraction of having Bryan bang his cartons around the hall. Also, Bev had one of those child safety gates in the office for when she brought her four-year-old son to work. I figured it would temporarily do to keep Skiball from roving too far.

"I'd sort of like some quiet right now," I said. "Later might be best."

"You got it."

I told him I'd appreciate that. Skiball *meh-eh-ehed*.

"Hey! What's that in there?" Bryan pointed to the pet carrier, bent to look inside. "Sky, wow, a cat!"

I think he expected that would come as a revelation.

"Yes," I said, "Skiball is a cat."

Bryan gave a nod.

"Skiball. Cool name," he said in an admiring tone. "Bet she's the one that belonged to your friend, huh? The poor old man who got killed."

I looked at him.

"How did you know?" I said.

"About your friend?" he said. "Could've been last night, a couple people told me what happened to him. And then after I got here today I heard it from some more people in the pressroom. And then—"

"Bryan," I said, "I was talking about the cat."

"Oh," he said. "I think that new reporter might've said something. You know, Mark? Or is it Matt? I forget."

"You mean Mike Ennis?"

"Right, yeah," Bryan said. "If he had a cool name like Skiball, I absolutely would've remembered it."

I didn't smile and his cheeks flushed a little.

"Sorry," he said. "But it isn't supposed to be top secret, is it? About the cat, that is. Because, Mike didn't really say anything to *me*. He was meeting with Gregg in editorial, and I was kind of walking past the door—"

I held up a hand to cut him short.

"That's okay, I was just curious," I said. Mike Ennis had started at the paper a few weeks earlier. A good-looking guy about my age—which is to say thirtyish—he pretty much kept to himself but always had a smile ready when we crossed paths. Word was that he'd been a crime reporter at the *Washington Post,* and it was a matter of ongoing speculation why he'd want to go from a major daily to our little paper . . . although I'd heard his family was from the Cape, which could have had something to do with it.

Anyway, whether I liked it or not, old Abe's murder was big news, and I wasn't surprised to hear that Mike and Gregg had been discussing it.

"Bryan," I said, my mystery solved, "I have to get to work."

He nodded and backed out of the entry.

"See you," he said. "And don't worry about the boxes."

"I won't," I said, and thanked him again, knowing they'd probably still be there in a month.

As Bryan whisked off down the corridor, I went to get the safety gate from where it was leaning against the wall, set it up in the doorway, put the pet carrier on floor, and opened it.

Skiball's head poked out first. Then the rest of her emerged.

"Eeeee!" she said.

"Yup, you're free," I said, and turned from the door.

Five minutes later I was sitting in front of a blank computer monitor. Ten minutes later it was still blank. Well, not quite. I'd gotten the name of my column, "Sky Writing," typed and centered above the blankness.

I sat some more, boldfaced the column's name, and assessed my progress. Then Skiball jumped up on my lap, put her front paws on the edge of the desk, and purred. After a while her mouth filled with spit and she started purring louder. I thought that meant she liked the title.

"Thanks, shorty," I said, and scratched the back of her neck.

Skiball swallowed some spit and let whatever was left in her mouth drool onto my arm. The wetness aside, I felt sort of flattered. It was a bonding moment for us.

We studied the title together. It always looked nice up at the top of the screen, and I was proud of it and thought it was kind of clever. Usually I followed it with a header about my subject for a particular installment of the column. Also usually I would set down what I hoped were my wryly amusing and insightful observations, framed as anecdotes about the people of Cape Ann. Throw in a cleaning tip, and you had the complete package.

It was work, but it was fun too, the best part being that it had a few fans besides just Skiball and me. In the three months since I'd turned in my first column, which had started out as a one-shot experiment, "Sky Writing" had developed a pretty decent following among readers of the paper—and, I'd been told, given its circulation a measurable jolt. On the basis of the positive response, Gregg had decided to make it a regular feature, squeezing enough out of his budget to have me do two columns a month at a couple of hundred bucks a pop. It was hardly enough to let me get out of the cleaning business, but I wasn't about to complain. In fact, I sometimes worried that my creative flow would get blocked if I couldn't channel it while setting a room straight.

In the office now, Skiball stretched her left forepaw toward the keyboard and plunked it down on the letter "n," keeping it there a few seconds so that the character repeated across my screen.

"Nnnnnnnnn," I said, reading the line aloud.

It didn't do much for me, but I couldn't come up with anything better. The problem was, I didn't feel very focused that afternoon—or wry or insightful, for that matter. I was still trying to absorb having lost a friend in a stunning and tragic way, and couldn't stop picturing him on the floor at the Millwood Inn. Who in town would have been capable of murdering Abe? Why would anyone have done it?

All I could think was that I didn't know what to think.

I sat for a while longer with Skiball on my lap. She was purring noisily and had made a very large, wet spit mark on my sleeve. Having expressed everything she could with the letter "n," she moved her paw over to the SHIFT key, moved it again, and added two lines' worth of colons to our piece. The pattern of double dots seemed to please her, or spark her curiosity, or both, because she immediately pushed off my lap and started swatting at them.

I lifted her off the desk and deposited her on the floor. Fair was fair. I really needed to put some effort of my own into our collaboration.

For her part, Skiball seemed content leaving the rest of the creative responsibilities to me. No sooner had I set her down than she found a paper clip on the carpet, flipped it up in the air, and started chasing it around the office.

A few uninspired minutes passed. And then a few more. I stared intently at my computer monitor and decided some of the colons would have to go. I didn't know what would replace them but felt that fifteen or twenty was redundant and that Skiball wouldn't mind my tweaking her prose.

I was about to hit the DELETE key when I heard a knock on the open door behind me, swiveled around in my chair, and saw Mike Ennis, the crime reporter, behind the child safety gate. Looking dapper in a tweed sport coat and gray trousers, he held a squirming, squealing Skiball in his hands—either that or a cat with an incredible resemblance to her, right down to the impeccable white paws.

"I think you misplaced something," Mike said.

I sat there with my face full of surprise, resisting the urge to look around the office as if he actually *might* have brought over a different cat.

Mike smiled. I assumed it was at my dopey expression.

"Guess your little friend here's an escape artist," he said. "I found her sitting on top of a copy machine."

Still at a loss, I got up and went to the door.

"Sorry," I said finally. "I don't know how she got out. Or even when she did, to be honest. But I guess she must've jumped over the gate."

Mike gave Skiball a pat on the head and handed her over to me.

"Meieeee," she said, sounding displeased at being passed around.

Mike smiled again. "She's very vocal."

"No kidding. Wait till she finds out she's going back in her pet carrier—trust me, you won't want to hear it."

We looked at each other across the gate.

"Thanks for snaring her," I said. "I'd hate to have Xeroxes of her furry butt circulate around the office."

Mike's smile broadened.

"That would be scandalous," he said.

This time I was the one who smiled.

"Well," I said, "I'd better get to work."

"Same here," Mike said.

He hesitated. I noticed his face had become serious.

"I'm covering the Abel Monahan story," he said.

"I know," I said.

"You do?"

"Bryan mentioned it," I said. "The kid from the Webmaster's office?"

"Oh, sure. With the studs and hoops."

I nodded.

"We were just talking a couple of minutes ago," I said.

"Oh."

"And he happened to tell me."

"Right, I got that," Mike said. "Anyway, what you did is very special."

"What I did?"

Mike motioned toward Skiball.

"Abe's cat," he said. "Chief Vega told me she was brought to a city shelter."

I nodded my sudden understanding.

"I went and picked her up this morning," I said with a dismissive flap of my hand. "Guess I've got a soft spot for manic but lovable bundles of trouble."

Mike was quiet for about thirty seconds, looking at me from his side of the gate.

"Give yourself credit," he said at last. "Abel obviously cared about the cat. And it says something that you went out of your way to take responsibility for her. These days, people forget what friendship is supposed to mean." He paused. "It would have been easy enough to figure she'd be cared for at the shelter. Nobody could even blame you."

I tried to answer, but my throat had clenched up. That may have been for the best, since I wasn't sure I would've known what to say if it hadn't.

Meanwhile, Mike had stayed put.

"Well," he went on. "Like you said, we're both busy."

I nodded.

"It's been a pleasure talking with you, though," he said. "I'd meant to do it sooner. But you know how it is . . ." A shrug. "I've been trying to get settled in, I suppose. New home, new job . . ."

I nodded again. Neither of us budged from the doorway.

"So," Mike said. His eyes lingered on mine. "I'm thinking maybe you'd like—that is, I was thinking *I'd* like to carry on our conversation outside the office."

I hefted Skiball in my arms and pressed her close.

"Say, Friday night," he said.

I held Skiball closer

"Over dinner," Mike said.

We stood there exchanging looks for what felt like an entire minute.

"Dinner," I said, finally managing to push a single word past my tongue.

Mike nodded.

"I know this Portuguese restaurant," he said. "It's got the best seafood, a casual atmosphere. And I'm close to its owners. We can't go wrong."

I stood there with my arms wrapped tightly around Skiball, still feeling as if my reactions were on time delay. I wondered if Mike was feeling sorry for me like everyone else in the office felt sorry for me. Then I wondered if he was asking me out to get an inside angle for his story. Last, I wondered if it was wrong of me to be wondering about someone who hadn't given me any reason at all to do it, but, on the contrary, had just said some of the sweetest and most thoughtful things I'd heard in longer than I could begin to remember.

I had no definite answers. Not for myself. But in spite of that, I realized I did have one for Mike.

"Sure," I said. "Dinner would be great."

Chapter 5

I was in Maplewood State Park, at the northern point of Pigeon Cove, jogging along one of the quarry trails and feeling conflicted. A big part of me was enjoying the bright morning sunshine and the fresh salt air of Ipswich Bay. Another part of me was still mired in grief over Mr. Monahan and trying to figure out why in the world anyone would want to hurt him—and what could have led to Bill Drecksel's falling-out with him on the Wing, something Chloe had told me Jessie still refused to inform the police about. Finally, a good-sized chunk of me was primed for my dinner date with Mike Ennis, but even that was a source of inner turmoil. Ever since I'd said yes to Mike, a sense of guilt had been slowly chipping away at my anticipation and making me uptight.

I hadn't thought for a second that I could work off that guilt like a few unwanted vanity pounds. But I did figure an early run would settle my mind, and there couldn't have been a better place for that than the quarries.

For more than a hundred years, starting in the mid-1800s, Pigeon Cove granite had been a building material used throughout the country and beyond. At least to hear it from the town elders, Harvard Square and the New York Stock Exchange would be full of rustic log cabins if not for our local stone, and the Panama Canal nothing more than a mucky drainage ditch. While that might have been a slight exaggeration, there's no doubt that granite quarrying was easily as important as shipbuilding to the Cove's early growth and remained a backbone of its economy until around 1930, when slowed urban development during the Great Depression and the increasing use of cement and steel-frame construction dealt the industry a double whammy.

One thing I've learned about New Englanders, though, is that they'll recoil in horror from any thought of wasting a resource. Austerity's in their DNA, and with it a deeply instilled imperative to reclaim and reuse. The owner of the quarries had known incredible success during his company's heyday, amassing a fortune so large that his heirs couldn't have squandered it if they'd tried. When business dried up, he'd granted a wide swath of land to the state for use as a public recreational area, including the excavation sites and over two hundred surrounding acres of untouched woods. Over many decades, the bay's currents had worn inlets into the rocky walls of the quarries, which ranged from shallow basins to yawning craters. Gradually filling with water from tidewater and underground springs, they became scenic attractions within the park, and, in the case of the shallower, low-sided tide pools, favorite bathing spots for townies.

Chloe had told me that skinny-dipping was the rage in Maplewood for years before peepers from Boston and elsewhere got wind of it and started to show up in droves with their binoculars. Things grew more uncomfortable when one of the Cove's more famous photographers, Benson Apple, was caught in the bushes snapping photos of male swimmers, and selling them to a Hollywood pop star for his personal voyeur's gallery. It wasn't long afterward that the few holdouts who'd continued bathing in the buff had reluctantly thrown on swimsuits. Well, except for Ed Blount, an eighty-seven-year-old watercolorist who's eccentric even by the Cove's laissez-faire standards. A militant nudist, Ed defiantly continues to strip down at the quarries and expose himself while painting on the front terrace of his Main Street home—much to the chagrin of neighbors and the police.

Jogging along in the park now, I glanced over my right shoulder at the sheer, 150-foot plunge of the largest quarry pit. The view was dizzily breathtaking, and I thought I'd take a moment to appreciate it before the trail swung off into a patch of blue spruces up ahead.

I could see gulls diving from the juts and ledges down below the crater's rim, where they perched waiting for the inbound tide to deliver their breakfast of fish, crabs, and brine shrimp. I didn't know how deep the water was at the bottom of the pit, but the current looked very brisk, with the breeze rippling its surface and chains of little wavelets lapping at the high, seamed walls of orange-brown granite, their crests white and foamy as they broke.

I moved on into the shade of the evergreens at a steady, rhythmic clip, wearing a black tank top, baggy lime-colored running shorts with a dandelion puff pattern, white Nike sneakers, and an exercise belt with a fanny pack and pouches for my cell phone, iPod, and water bottle. The digital music player was turned off so I could soak up the tranquil sights and sounds of the park. Maybe they would help ease the tightness in my stomach and maybe they wouldn't. But it had seemed worth a shot.

The guilt was the worst part for me, the most difficult thing to deal with. I knew the reason for it, and also I knew that any attempt to deny or suppress it would only feed into it and make it worse. Whatever I did to push ahead with my life, it was something I couldn't just pry off my back. It would stay or leave me in its own good time, and I could only do my best to carry it without letting it weigh my feet down into the ground.

I had adored my late husband from the day we met. We'd shared six wonderful years of marriage, and dreams for the future that held no room for the possibility of Paul dying at thirty-seven. He'd taken good care of himself and never smoked a cigarette in his life. He shouldn't have gotten lung cancer. But he did, who knows why, it hadn't mattered. When we found out, we told ourselves he would beat it, and kept telling ourselves that almost right up until the cancer beat him.

The idea of being without Paul had never occurred to me. I had loved him too much to imagine it. And after he was gone, and being without him had become my reality, I'd still loved him too much to consider everything that went along with it—such as having another man ask me out to dinner, and accepting his invitation, and looking forward to being with him more than I'd looked forward to anything in ages.

I'd told myself my date with Mike wasn't romantic. Wasn't really even a date, but a couple of workplace acquaintances being sociable. Back at the office after Mike asked me out, I'd been chock-full of such clarifications. My heart was racing with excitement only because of the unexpected break from routine. Sure. The same went for the tingles I felt from my shoulders down to my fingertips. Righteo. I'd been a married woman for six years, and hadn't quite stopped thinking of myself as a married woman, which made it an adjustment going out with a guy—even in a social, nonromantic, nondating sort of way. Uh-huh, easy to explain.

But about two minutes later, I'd started thinking

about what outfit I would wear, and planning what I would do with my hair, and realized that I had called my own bluff. It left me feeling like I was sixteen again, which was the last time I'd tried to fool myself about my reasons for wanting to be alone with a member of the opposite sex.

His name was Scott Lyman. I was a high school sophomore, and he was in the senior class and a couple of years older than me. Once, Scott got tickets to a rock concert about a hundred miles from our town, and asked me to go with him, and said that he'd book a motel room so that we wouldn't have to drive home in the dark. We'd have separate beds, and everything would be pure and innocent. I wasn't sure either of us believed it for a minute, but it sounded all right to my ears.

I did my best to sell that line to my parents. I'd already sold myself on it, at least provisionally—which is to say that I figured it would hold true unless, for instance, Scott and I checked into our motel room and realized there was some mixup in our booking arrangements. That, shocker of shockers, we didn't get the separate beds we'd requested, but a double bed instead! If that happened, and room service was slow or unavailable at the late hour we'd be arriving, what would we do? Unless one of us slept on the floor, which seemed kind of unfair, I supposed we'd climb into our room's double bed with the intention of staying on opposite sides of the mattress, understanding there was always a chance, however slight, that one of us might accidentally roll on top of the other once the lights went out . . . Hey, people *did* toss around in their sleep, didn't they? And after that, well, who knew? Human biology being what it was, your grip on the controls wasn't fail-safe. You could come into a situation with the best intentions, but it was impossible to plan for *everything.*

When I presented this arrangement to my parents—minus the hypothetical single-bed-double-bed-mixup scenario—I insisted that I liked Scott, and that we had a good rapport, but were just sort of hanging out a lot, as opposed to being a couple in the true sense of the word, and that this was why they should give me their okay. I admit I'd even tried playing to their vestigial flower child sensibilities and spouted some dopiness about our relationship transcending the physical. *It's about us utterly and totally getting into each other's heads*, I'd told them.

Maybe if I was a smoother operator, I'd have kept in mind that they'd named me Sky because I was conceived under the wild blue yonder while they were living in a commune somewhere in Northern California, the two of them out in a sun-soaked glade utterly getting into other's heads and various anatomical etceteras with their tie-dyed shirts and bell-bottoms tossed over a nearby branch. It might also have paid to remember that their fateful jaunt had happened a bunch of years before they got married.

Be that as it may, Mom hadn't had much peace and love in her eyes after I asked the question.

Instead, she had lobbed a different one right back at me.

"Do you kiss him?" she said pointedly.

I looked at her with my mouth wide open.

"What do you mean?" I said.

She'd puckered her lips and made a wet, smoochy noise.

"Do you two k-i-s-s?" she'd said, spelling it out. "Be honest."

I stood there, yawped some more, and eventually nodded, knowing I had blown it.

"If you kiss him, and he kisses you back, you are a couple," Mom said. "And if you are a couple, you are *not* sharing a motel room on my watch."

And that was that. I hadn't been kidding anybody back then. Nor was I kidding myself now. Silly and adolescent as it sounded, the question still got to the root of what was bothering me. All I had to do was make a simple word substitution, swapping "do" for "would."

Would I kiss Mike?

It seemed way to early to think about that. Why suppose there'd be any kind of romantic spark? For either of us? Maybe the date would even turn out to be a snoozer. But for the sake of argument, say it didn't. Say it went swimmingly and we hit it off . . .

Would I kiss him?

I didn't know. Didn't even know why I was worrying about it. I only knew it wasn't something I had ruled out.

Hence, the guilt had become an unwanted, unwieldy piggyback rider during my morning run.

I'd kept going on the path as it left the trees for a thicket of dark green shrubs and then bent back toward the quarry, where it led past the grout pile on the northwestern side. Constituted of waste granite that had been hauled and dumped there during the quarry's active years—the stones ranged from gravel chips to huge cracked blocks—it rose near the edge of the pit in a small hill, making a perfect overlook from which you could gaze across the wide mouth of the pit to the headlands and the open sea beyond.

There were two men over by the granite heap, near one of those informational signs for visitors who are curious about the background of what they're seeing. One was a thin, white-haired grandfatherly type. He held a fawn-colored greyhound on a retractable leash, the dog standing very still beside him while he read the park sign. His companion—the human one—was much younger, maybe thirty-five or so. He'd been gazing out over the quarry as I approached, but then I saw him turn his head in my direction, and guessed it was because he'd heard me emerge from the thicket. Tall and square-shouldered, his blond hair worn in a barely outgrown buzz cut, he had on a pair of dark wraparound sunglasses.

As I got closer, the white-haired man looked up from the sign and also shifted his attention my way.

"Hi there, doll!" he said with a wave. "Now

you're somebody who knows how to start the day right."

I smiled. "Oh?"

The man took a deep breath and looked up at the sky.

"Fresh air, morning sunshine," he said. "Ain't nothing in the wide world can beat it."

"You won't hear me argue with that," I said, a little breathless from exertion.

I'd come almost up to where he stood and was about to trot on past when his dog stepped onto the trail in front of me, bringing me to a screeching halt.

"Sorry," the man said, tugging on its leash. "Don't mind my Rosie, she's a friendly gal."

His Rosie was also a gal who refused to budge from the middle of the trail. Instead she assumed a play position, her head low, ears tucked back, her tail wagging.

I slowly extended my hand for her to sniff. She licked it once to confer the official canine mark of approval, moved lengthwise against me, and pressed her body against my legs.

The white-haired man chuckled. His blue golf shirt, perfectly creased tan trousers, and brown loafers—classic day-tripper couture for the senior set—made me think of Old Abe.

"Now you got trouble," he said. "She gives you the lean, that's *amore*."

Rosie pressed harder, as if in confirmation, her penny-colored eyes regarding me with good-natured curiosity. This made me an object of undivided interest on the trail, since both her owner and his companion were also looking at me.

Then Rosie nuzzled me again, leaning so heavily I was afraid she'd bowl me over. I knelt to scratch under her chin—and lower my center of gravity so I'd have a shorter distance to fall if she knocked me onto my backside. She must have weighed seventy or eighty pounds to my one-twenty.

"Wow," I said, glancing up at the white-haired man. "She's solid muscle."

He nodded.

"Rosie's a retired racer. A money winner, y'know? She gets to be four years old, loses a step, they want to put her down."

I frowned. I'd heard a few things about the treatment of racing dogs, and just about all of it was dreadful.

"Did you get her from a rescue center?"

The white-haired man shook his head.

"Buddy of mine's a trainer," he said. "Rosie here was his favorite, and he sorta took a shine to her and hooked us up."

I stayed crouched on my knees and scratched her another minute.

"You're a real sweetheart, aren't you?" I said in the idiotic cooing voice people reserve for kids and pets. "Lucky thing you found yourself a such nice dad."

The white-haired man flapped his hand.

"I'm the lucky one," he said. "Ain't a better pal around than Rosie."

I smiled, reminded of what Mike had said about my adopting Skiball. *Give yourself credit . . . it says something that you went out of your way to take responsibility for her.*

"I guess," I said, "it was luck twice over."

The white-haired man returned my smile.

"Yeah," he said. "I like how that sounds."

I stood, backstepping before Rosie could attach herself to me again. My legs had tightened up a little from crouching and I bounced on my knees to flex them.

"Well, I'd better go finish my jog," I said to the white-haired man. "Enjoy the day."

"Same to you." He chuckled again. "Tell you something, doll. I'd known it'd make a pretty lady like you think I'm such a swell guy, I probably would've brought home a grey thirty years ago!"

Behind him, his companion offered a small nod.

"Don't be fooled, he's had dogs all his life," he said. I realized those were the first words he'd said since I'd stopped at Checkpoint Rosie. "When it comes to my uncle, a simple nice-to-meet-you is never enough. He doesn't know when to quit."

Which I thought was a sort of nasty thing for him to say. Not so much to me, but about the grandfatherly—or maybe I should say avuncular, now that I knew their relationship—old man.

I turned up the trail, not reading a whole lot into it. They were obviously from out of town. Back when I lived in New York, a woman alone in the park might've gotten uneasy if a strange guy started talking to her. Codgers included, it pains me to say. Maybe he just didn't want me to get any wrong ideas about his uncle. Or maybe I *was* reading too much into it.

Some people were chatty, and others weren't, and clearly the blond man wasn't.

No big deal, I thought, and jogged on ahead.

Chapter 6

"Are you sure you can do this right now?"

"I'm sure," I said.

"Because I wouldn't want your other clients feeling snubbed."

"Don't worry. They won't mind."

"I hope so. You've had enough on your hands these past few days—"

"Trust me, Jess. It's not a problem," I said, wondering how many more reassurances she'd need to hear.

An hour after I finished my morning jog, I was with Jessie Barton in the August Moon, her little women's clothing boutique next door to Drecksel's Diner on the Wing. My regular twice-monthly appointment to clean the shop's clothing racks wasn't scheduled for another four days, but I'd gotten the brainstorm of pulling a switch with another of my steady gigs, this one at the Hobbs Native American Art Gallery in the town center. Longmont and Heidi Hobbs had just returned from an extended buying trip to New Mexico, and they'd been perfectly all right with the change when I phoned to ask about it. In fact, they'd seemed kind of relieved to know I wouldn't be bumping around the place with my cleaning kit while they unpacked and organized their new exhibition.

For her part, Jessie initially met my offer to push up my visit with delight—though she'd started wavering by the time I arrived. But while it was a pain trying to convince her I wasn't putting myself in a hole, I had to appreciate her concern. There really was a lot of work to be done. She'd pulled a dozen extra chrome rack units from her basement in preparation for a big delivery of summer merchandise—bathing suits, sarongs, peasant skirts, batik blouses, and so forth—and most of them were kind of grungy from the long winter's storage. The new stock was set to arrive later that day, and she wanted the racks to be gleaming before everything was put out on view.

As for me, I'd had a secret agenda for wanting to shuffle my jobs. One that had come to me in a flash toward the end of my run in the park.

In short, I wanted information.

Now Jessie stood there in the middle of the sales floor, looking chicly put together in a tight shoulderless blouse and flowing black chiffon skirt with the Parisian skyline, Eiffel Tower and all, printed front and back in panorama. Her long silence told me I almost had her convinced.

"Jess, don't give me a seizure," I said. "Since I'm already here, how about I get started?"

She gave her button nose a thoughtful tap, and then folded her arms under her silicon-enhanced breasts. I almost felt like I was watching a show-and-tell. Jessie treated herself to a plastic surgeon's visit every year on her birthday and had been sporting the pixyish nose since her last trip, in celebration of her thirty-seventh. The year before, Jessie's gift to herself had been the breast implants showcased by her figure-hugging top. Between birthdays she'd undergone a microdermabrasion that had yielded her a creamy white complexion, and a micropigmentation procedure resulting in wine-colored borders around her lips. The lip tone had been selected from her doctor's extensive pigment collection, coordinating well with a thick, curly tumble of auburn hair that was not only Jessie's best asset, but happened to be all natural, which I always felt was kind of ironic.

Jessie was very candid about her plastic surgeries and had readily admitted that the last two outpatient procedures were a minor splurge that coincided with her ex's remarriage to a younger woman—though she'd fallen short of saying she'd had them done as tweaks to her self-esteem.

I personally didn't think Jessie owed anybody explanations about what she chose to do with her body. She was a grown woman who probably had more of her original, un-redesigned parts than most teenagers nowadays—and even if she didn't, that was her own business. But she absolutely had something to explain on a different front, and I wanted to nudge it out of her. I was glad when she gave me a look that indicated I might get my chance.

Sighing, Jessie nodded toward the display racks clustered against the back wall.

"They're very dull," she said.

"I figured."

"And dusty."

"Mm-hmm."

"And some of them have smear marks from I-know-not-what," Jessie said.

I couldn't have asked for a better opening. My bag of tricks was conveniently at my feet, and I bent and groped inside it for a minute. Then I frowned and groped around some more, picking stuff up, putting it back, making a rackety theatrical production out of it. After another thirty seconds, I looked up at Jessie and pulled my lips farther down my face.

"Oh, brother," I said.

"Is anything wrong?"

I nodded.

"Not enough lemons," I said.

"What?"

"I forgot my lemons," I said. "There's a slice in some plastic wrap. But I should've brought a lot more. What with all these racks."

"I'm confused," Jessie said.

"Lemons can't be beat for polishing chrome," I explained. "Rub a wedge over a section, wipe it with a damp cleaning cloth, and the juice cuts right through the dirt and sticky stuff."

"Oh."

"You've seen me do it before, Jess."

"I suppose I have, now that you mention it . . ."

"But it won't work if I don't have enough lemons to go around," I said, leading her right along.

Jessie tapped her dot of a nose again.

"Bill Drecksel's got plenty of lemons, you know," she said. "I'm sure he could spare a few from his restaurant."

I straightened. She couldn't have played into my hands any better.

"Drecksel's restaurant," I said. "That's an idea."

"Great."

"Except," I said, "I just can't bring myself to ask Bill Drecksel for anything."

Jessie had returned to looking baffled.

"You can't?"

"I can't."

"Why not?"

"I'm uncomfortable with it."

"You are?"

"I am."

"Sky, I know Bill's got a reputation as a cheapskate, but if you're only asking for *lemons*—"

"It's not about lemons," I said, and paused a second. "It's about Abe Monahan. I hear Bill threatened him the day he was killed, and that gives me the creeps."

Jessie's lips tightened at the corners.

"Chloe, damn her. I should've known," she said

half under her breath. "Next time I work out a song list I'll do it without her input, which wasn't so terrific anyway. The La-dee-das are about a melodic expression of our womanhood. But I give her that atrocious Springsteen number without a peep of complaint, and she's got the nerve to come back at me with reservations about 'Long Island Cowboy' by Red Molly—"

"I didn't say I heard anything from Chloe," I interrupted before she could stray too far off topic, thinking that must have been epidemic among the La-dee-das.

Jessie sighed.

"Sky, I'm the only person who was around when Bill and Abe had words. And Chloe's the only person I told about it. So it stands to reason *she* has to be the one who told you."

I shrugged.

"What if she did, Jess? Chloe's my best friend. We confide all the time, and she knows how I felt about Old Abe. What'd be wrong with her telling me?"

"What's wrong is that I didn't want Chloe to share it with you. Or anyone else."

"Did you make it clear their argument was supposed to be a secret?"

Jessie pursed her lips.

"Not clear enough, obviously," she said after a second. "But the fact is I didn't want anybody to know. Just like I didn't want Bruce Springsteen in our repertoire. Twice I let Chloe have her way, and both times I get a swift kick in return."

I hurried her along. "So you haven't spoken to Chief Vega yet?"

"No," Jesse said. "And as I'm sure Chloe's also informed you, I don't plan on speaking to him."

"How come?"

"Because Bill didn't do anything to Abel Monahan."

"Besides threaten him?" I said, and looked her straight in the eye.

Jessie stared quietly back at me.

"There weren't any threats," she said.

"None?"

She gave an adamant head shake, tossing her jungle of red hair around her shoulders.

"Bill's a big talker," she said. "All he really did was bark at Abe."

"Then why won't you tell me what he said?"

Jessie shrugged.

"Check the definition of hurtful gossip," she said. "Certain remarks just shouldn't be repeated out of context. That can lead to mistaken impressions."

I wanted to say that leaving them to the imagination just might be worse, but bit my tongue. I was afraid I'd hit a wall with Jess, and decided I had myself to blame for coming on too strong. Then I remembered something Chloe had mentioned about Jessie the day before and thought it might point to a less confrontational way of drawing her out.

"Jess," I said, "I admire your devotion to Bill.

We can disagree whether it's wise under the circumstances. But it's kind of nice to see firsthand."

She cocked her head sideways, her mane spilling over her bare shoulder.

"What do you mean, 'firsthand'?"

"Well, it's sort of common knowledge in town that you'll do anything to protect him," I said.

Her eyes widened.

"It is?" she said. "Common knowledge?"

"Oh, definitely," I lied with a shrug, wanting to take some heat off Chloe. "Everybody thinks it's overboard, but very sweet."

Jessie's head remained at a puzzled tilt.

"I can't believe this," she said. "Can you give me a for instance?"

I shrugged again.

"Take how you always rave about Bill's coffee to tourists," I said. "It's pretty obvious you're trying to drum up business for him."

Jessie gave me a defiant look. "I happen to love Bill's coffee," she said testily.

I spread my hands.

"See, Jess, that's what I mean. Remember when Rita Mercer's reading club came in last time I was here? They'd just had breakfast at Bill's, and were all grumbling, and Rita told us it was because—"

"She said his coffee tasted like a monkey's bathwater, I remember." Jessie flapped her hand in dismissal. "But who cares about her opinion? Since when did Rita and the Bookworms get to be such connoisseurs?"

"I'm not saying they are," I replied. "Still,

you've got to admit, Drecksel's Special Blend does tend to be on the watery side."

Jessie was looking at me. "The weaker the better. I can drink it by the gallon without getting the jitters. Or making a dozen trips to the bathroom. Without Bill's coffee I'd be stuck drinking decaf." She wrinkled her nose. "Nothing's worse than that."

I decided to try pushing her buttons at random. With any luck I'd jab the right one.

"Jess, like you said, what do people's opinions matter? Why care if they speculate about your relationship with Bill? Or think he sometimes takes advantage of you?"

"Relationship! Advantage! What did I just tell you about gossip? Bill's old enough to be my father!"

"You don't need to explain. Your personal life's your own. If you can't tell me what happened between Bill and Mr. Monahan, I'll just have to accept that you've got your reasons."

Jessie stared at me with consternation. I didn't know exactly what I'd said that had gotten to her and couldn't have cared less. Just so long as she opened up.

"If I tell you," she said, "promise you'll let me be the one to tell Chief Vega."

I looked at her.

"You'll really go to him?" I said in a firm tone.

"I will," Jessie said. "It might have to wait just a bit. I have the merchandise coming in this afternoon, and I've got a few odds and ends to take care of tonight. But I'll stop by the police station tomorrow. If you'll promise."

I wasn't thrilled about the delay and had a hunch Jessie might use it as wiggle room for avoiding Vega when the time came. But I gave her my word anyway. What choice was there? I'd gone pretty far on blind improvisation and didn't intend to press my luck.

Jessie's eyes had drifted toward the front of the shop, as if she wanted to be positive nobody would enter while she was talking. That didn't make sense, since her door was locked and the store wouldn't open for another hour. But it was my distinct impression.

"Okay," she said at last. She'd returned her attention to me. "You know the lot Abe owned out at the south end of town? That field where he was always heading to putter with his stone wall?"

I nodded. "Of course."

"Well, it borders on some land that Bill inherited from relatives a while ago. And that happens to be where he wants to build one of those yuppie condo sprawls. You know the type."

I looked at her. I hadn't heard anything about Bill's ambitions as a developer—or his ownership of the land next to Abe's, come to think of it. But with real estate prices having gone through the roof in Boston's immediate area, it was impossible to miss the swank bedroom communities that were the rage all over the north coast. So far, however, Pigeon Cove's matchlessly snailish and contentious government committees had resisted the building trend. And while I vaguely recalled some news about a south end rezoning proposal right around the time I moved up from New York, it hadn't seemed important enough to stick in my mind. Furthermore, I was pretty sure it didn't involve Bill Drecksel.

"Are you saying Bill wanted to buy Abe's plot?" I asked.

Jessie nodded.

"He was on him with an offer for the past year," she said, and dropped her voice to a low, confidential tone. Again, I got the weird feeling she was afraid of unseen eavesdroppers. "Several offers, actually. I'm sure you can imagine how Abe would have reacted."

I could, and it made me shake my head.

"Abe loved his piece of land," I said. "There's no chance he would've sold."

Jessie was nodding again.

"Which was the problem in a nutshell," she said. "Those two used to be buddy-buddy. But it annoyed Bill that Abe was holding up his blockbuster deal, especially since he lived out of town and had no intention of doing anything with the property. Aside from finishing that wall of his."

I let that sink in a minute.

"So Bill was mad about Abe's turndown," I said.

"It was just frustration," Jessie said. "His heart's set on the condo project. He even paid some computer graphics outfit a small fortune to work up a picture of what it'll look like—you can see it for yourself in his restaurant."

I shook my head.

"The whole thing sounds pretty bottom line," I said. "No sale, no friendship."

Jessie shrugged. "Maybe so. You know how volatile things can be when business and money enter the mix. Though Bill did tell me the last offer he presented was exceptionally generous."

I didn't like the sound of that. It seemed to imply Abe had been somehow obliged to bite at whatever Bill dangled on his hook.

"You can't force someone to sell," I said. "That's bullying, not business."

Jessie paused for a beat.

"Sky," she said, "I hate to tell you, but Abe wasn't perfection incarnate."

"Huh?" I said, not quite liking the implication there either. "I don't catch your meaning."

Jessie shrugged.

"No disrespect to his memory," she said, "but he had a way of antagonizing people."

I blinked.

"Are we talking about the same Abel Monahan?" I said. "Because nobody was more well liked than the Abe I knew."

Jessie looked at me, sighing deeply. "Why don't you ask your client Stu Redman about that?"

"Stu the bookseller?"

"Right."

"Stu didn't like Abe?"

"Stu detested Abe."

"Detested?"

Jessie nodded. "From what I could tell, yes."

"*Why?*"

"I think it had something to do with Abe letting a seagull poop on an old book, you'd have to ask Stu for the details," Jessie said. "And while you're at it, you can go talk to Noel Lawless."

"Noel the überfeminist?"

"Who told me Abe was an unbearable wretch," Jessie said with another nod. "Of course, Noel isn't just a glass half-empty sort of person. She also figures somebody must have *spit* in the glass. But still . . . remember last year, when she was talking to you and Abe at Chloe's Christmas party?"

I nodded.

"Well, the nicest thing she could say about Abe afterward was that he bored her to death talking about old houses and building rock walls," Jessie said. "Then, I think it must've been a week or so later, Noel came into the shop ranting and raving that he'd had the nerve—her exact word—to tell her to watch her step leaving the house because the front porch looked slippery."

My mouth dropped open.

"Let me get this straight," I said. "That made her *mad*?"

"Furious," Jessie said. "She took it as an insult. As if Abe was so much of a chauvinist, he felt Noel was too stupid and helpless to figure out she needed to be careful on her own."

I blinked. That last news flash had my head spinning.

"Okay, let's back up a second," I said. "You still haven't told me about the other morning. What Bill shouted at Abe."

Jessie looked at me, tapped her nose, exhaled.

"I suppose a deal's a deal," she said. "If you insist."

I nodded.

"Bill threw him out of his restaurant," she said, with a second gust of breath. "They were out on the sidewalk when I heard them going at it."

"And?"

"First Bill called Abe a stubborn bastard who wasn't welcome to his coffee anymore," Jessie said. "Then he told Abe to get his crummy old rattletrap car on the highway and drive back to Florida."

She hesitated. I took it as a sign that there was more, and wound my hand to urge her on.

Jessie stayed quiet another second or two before she finally gave me an acquiescent shrug.

"Then Bill swore that if he ever laid eyes on Abe again, he'd crack his head open like a jumbo egg and scramble his brains all over Pigeon Cove," she said.

Chapter 7

"Jessie wants my lemons? No problem!" Bill Drecksel said with a tug on his brown walrus mustache. "I got a big, juicy handful she's welcome to grab any time, ha-ha!"

He gave a wink that was meant to look roguish, wanting to make sure his double entendre hadn't been lost on me. Such high-flying wit—gee, you never knew when it would soar over someone's head.

Good thing for me I'd gone to grade school.

I stood across the lunch counter from Drecksel and tried to figure out why I was there. Back in the August Moon, I'd overstated—not to say faked—my unwillingness to face him so I could prompt—not to say manipulate—Jessie into revealing his angry final words to Old Abe. But that reluctance had become very genuine once I'd learned what they were . . . and the reason why they'd been spoken.

Moments afterward, I had pushed aside my res-

ervations and marched straight from the August
Moon to Drecksel's Diner. Until Jessie told me
about their clash, I'd found it hard to believe Bill
could have held any real animosity toward Abe.
In my mind, nobody could have felt that way
about him. But now that belief had been rocked
to the core. Bill, Stu Redman, Noel Lawless . . .
could *all* of them have disliked and resented him?
And if so, how many others might he have rubbed
the wrong way?

I didn't know what to think, or where to turn
my suspicions. I'd been plenty upset for starters,
and going to see Bill Drecksel had worsened
things. Now that I was at the diner, I wasn't even
sure what I hoped to accomplish beyond my
stated goal of picking up a few lemons—something
that Jessie, to her credit, had offered to do for me.
Why was I putting myself through it?

Bill stood regarding me over the counter as all
this went through my mind. A large, bald man in
his fifties wearing a plaid shirt and jeans under
his splattered white cook's apron, Bill fancied himself as a strappingly macho and eternally youthful
kind of guy. When I first met him he'd had a full
head of hair and no mustache, but as the top of
his lawn started to visibly thin, he'd countered
that assault on his vanity with a scorched-earth
policy and shaved his scalp. His habit of polishing
it to a bright luster came later on, as did the bushy
whiskers that I guessed were an overcompensa-
tion for his loss of locks.

"Listen, Sky, I want to be serious," he said, leaning forward on his elbow. "I know you've had a rough spell. What with . . . ah, you know, that lousy experience you had at the Millwood. So how about a little coffee while you're here? On the house."

I managed not to gag at the proposition. Probably Bill was just being decent. Maybe Jessie was right and he'd been all bark and no bite the day Abe was killed. But in my raw emotional state, I almost could have believed that his offer to put Drecksel's Special Blend into my system meant he had it in for me too.

"No thanks," I said. "Nice of you to ask, though."

"You positive? It's piping hot in the urn."

"Don't tempt me." What was next, an anthrax latte? Still, I wanted to sound convincingly appreciative. "I've already had my morning dose of caffeine."

Bill slumped with disappointment, and it was easy to figure out why. With the exception of Jessie, I couldn't think of a single townie who would even want to sniff his coffee, let alone put it down his or her throat—and it might be another hour before the first unwary day-trippers drifted in. He would eventually foist his brew on someone, but meanwhile it would languish in the pot.

"Well, you change your mind, I got a cup waiting for you," Bill said resignedly. "Hold on a minute and I'll bring some of those lemons."

I waited as he moved down the counter and started groping around inside a refrigerated bin.

The place was quiet, its only customers the Beaufort twins, Beulah and Abigail, who were in a booth over to my left sharing a single bowl of cream of wheat. I made chance eye contact with one of them—I think it was Beulah—and waved hello to her, a gesture that got me a pinched little smile in return. The sisters lived together in an old house on Plum Street, and neither had ever married, or even dated as far as anyone knew. I always thought of them as sort of cobwebby, and had heard rumors of people turning to fossil dust at the sight of them.

Well, okay, that last part's a slight exaggeration. But I could practically feel my eyeballs drying up before I shifted them to the diner's walls, which were decorated with a local illustrator's pencil sketches of old-fashioned sailing ships. Drawings of schooners and clipper ships hung above the row of luncheonette booths behind me. A gallery of smaller vessels was mounted above the counter. There was a Norfolk wherry rigged with a single big sail, an English brig, a tubby Brighton hog boat, each with an identifying plate at the bottom of its frame. Although the picture I was searching for wasn't among them, I couldn't help but pause to admire their graceful, flowing style and authentic detail. It struck me that Bill's taste in artwork was surprisingly better than his taste in coffee. And his sense of humor.

A minute or two passed. Bill reached for a paper bag and started picking lemons from the bin. Meanwhile, I looked around some more and quickly found what I'd wanted to check out.

On the wall behind the register, encased in frameless Plexiglas, was a wide, full-color computer-generated drawing of several clapboard and shingle town houses—the complex surrounded by landscaped drives, gently curving walkways, and manicured grass islands and lawns. It took me about half a second to conclude that this was the digital graphic of Bill's planned condo development.

"Fabulous, huh?" Bill said from his side of the counter. He'd brought over the bag of lemons, put it down on the counter between us, and turned toward the picture.

"Very," I said, trying to sound simultaneously impressed and clueless. "If you don't mind my asking, what is it?"

Bill spread his arms expansively at his sides.

"Getaway Groves, the condominiums of your dreams!" he declared in a ringing tone. " 'Grand ocean views for the superior few' is our motto."

I continued to play dumb.

"Wow," I said. "Are they on the Cape?"

"Right now they're still in here." Bill tapped his shiny bald head. "But soon's I straighten a couple things out—me and my investment partner, that is—they'll be the south end's main attraction."

I looked at him. "You mean they're going up in Pigeon Cove?"

Bill nodded.

"We're gonna start with twenty-five units," he said. "Figure we top out at maybe forty, fifty, it depends."

"Depends on what?" I asked. "Sales?"

Bill shook his head.

"Sales won't be a problem, it's all how many acres wind up available to us," he said, and fell into a momentary silence. Then he thoughtfully ruffled a finger over his mustache and started reverberating with enthusiasm again. "The condos start at seven rooms and go to eleven. But let me tell you, Getaway Groves'll be jam-packed with luxury features no matter what size place you buy. There's cathedral ceilings, fireplaces, decks, Jacuzzi saunas—we're even using local granite for the kitchen countertops. And you want amenities? How's private tennis courts, stables, swimming pools, and a golf course! It'll even have its own zip code!" Bill grinned proudly and spread his arms again. "Imagine a world in a gift-wrapped box! A whole wonderful world! And it isn't too unaffordable if a person has a decent income! Or in your case finds a yuppie boyfriend that's got one, hey-ooh!"

Bill's *hey-ooh* told me the remark had been meant as a joke, and I let it slide. Besides, I'd thought about something else he'd just said and was wondering if I could get him to talk more about it without coming off like a snoop.

"How about if there aren't enough acres?" I asked.

"Huh? What do you mean?"

"For instance, if you couldn't acquire the land to build those tennis courts. Or stables. Didn't you say that could be an issue?"

Bill went back to ruffling his mustache. Outside, the morning sun had angled its light down over the street, and as it slanted over Bill through the restaurant's plate-glass window, I noticed for the first time that his formerly solid-brown whiskers had become smudged with traces of gray, giving them a dull, rusty sort of appearance overall.

"You want to make things happen, you figure out how. Nothing complicated about it," he said after a bit, and then became quiet again.

I looked at him and sensed he'd gotten a little disconcerted. Or maybe I was just projecting. What reason would he have to feel that way? He couldn't know that Jessie had told me about his argument over Abe's wooded lot, and probably wouldn't worry about it, considering how tight they were. But he did seem more subdued than he had a minute ago.

Then a Beaufort twin I guessed might be Abigail broke the silence. "Mr. Drecksel, may we have some fresh milk while the farina's hot?" she creaked from her booth. "And I've decided I would like a soft-boiled egg as well. Shelled and with an extra dish for my sister, please."

"Yes, ma'am, right with you. I'm just finishing up a take-out order." Bill said with another one of his compulsive winks. He lifted a paper cup from the stack behind him, filled it from the coffee urn, covered it with a plastic lid, and then pushed

it across the counter along with the bag of lemons.
"Tell Jessie I hope she has a great day," he said,
apparently over whatever real or imagined funk
he'd slipped into. "And that I'm sending the coffee to help her start it out right."

I took the bag and thanked him, taking a last
glance at the conceptual graphic of Getaway
Groves. I wasn't sure that I'd learned anything
new from my foray to the restaurant, but I headed
out the door thinking there were some new things
I needed to learn . . . although I wasn't sure what
they were either. Which I suppose qualified me
as mixed up in a new and different way. *Ha-ha,
hey-ooh.*

I stepped onto the sidewalk and had no sooner
turned toward Jessie's than my cell phone bleeped.
I paused in the streaming sunlight, shifted the bag
around so I could reach into my purse for it,
flipped it open, and saw Margaret Millwood's
name on the screen.

I smiled. She'd rung me at least twice a day
since Abe's murder to see how I was doing—and
to let me know about a gathering she'd planned
in his honor. She was calling it an "hour of re-
membrance," and had invited all of Abe's
friends to show up at his lot. It would be tough,
I knew. But at the same time I loved the idea and
knew it would be something Abe would have
appreciated . . . and, maybe, that some of us in
town needed.

"Hi, Marge," I said. "Hope you've had your
morning walk, because it's beautiful out."

My upbeat tone surprised both of us.

"You sound better today," she said.

"Guess I feel better," I said, thinking that leaving Drecksel's Diner must have accounted for at least part of it. "Feel okay, in fact."

"You're a resilient one, Sky," Marge said. "I wonder—that is, would you be able to drop by the inn? I need to talk to you about something."

The prospect of visiting the Millwood made me hesitate. I hadn't been there since Abe died, and felt I needed time to gird myself.

"I'm neck-deep in work right now," I said. "How about we do it tomorrow morning—" I interrupted myself. That was when Marge had arranged for Abe's ceremony. "No, wait, I guess that's out."

"Yes it is. But before lunchtime today would be perfect," Marge said. "I realize this is terribly short notice, darling. But I need a tremendous favor, and would rather not ask it over the phone."

I considered that. I desperately wanted to stall Marge, and had every excuse I needed to do that. The day was going to be a total blitz. I had the fixtures at the Autumn Moon to clean, and then another job around noon, and I'd blocked out an hour or so in the evening for my column. Also, I wanted to drive down to the health food store in Gloucester for some natural cat treats Chloe had told me they'd put on a one-day sale. But when it came down to it, I didn't feel I could refuse. Marge was more than my best client. She was a friend who sounded like she had an urgent reason for wanting to see me.

"Okay, I'll be over around eleven thirty," I said, and got off the phone.

Back at the Autumn Moon, I hurriedly started in on the clothing racks while Jessie sipped her free coffee and oohed and aahed about how tasty it was. The lemon juice got the dirt off the chrome easily enough, and I was finished with my work in a little over an hour—or would have been if I'd managed to avoid making still *more* work for myself.

Naturally, I didn't come close to avoiding it. I was putting a shine on my final rack when I noticed that Jessie had picked some lilacs from her yard and set them around the shop in a couple of blue glass vases. They looked and smelled nice, but the vases were kind of grungy inside, so I took a few extra minutes to clean them, removing the flowers, putting them a sink full of water to keep them from wilting, then pouring some warm tap water into the vases and dropping a denture tablet in each one.

"Let the water sit in the vases for about half an hour," I told Jessie as I was packing up. "Then dump it, pour in some fresh water, and stick the lilacs back in—the vases will sparkle."

Jessie seemed appreciative, judging from the air kisses she flurried around my cheeks.

And then I left the shop and sped over to the Millwood in my Honda, where I barely had time to pull into a spot out front before Marge came waddling down from the porch.

"Sky, I can't believe you're here so soon!" she said as I allowed her to lead me inside by the wrist. "You weren't supposed to arrive for a while yet."

. I sat down in the parlor, looked at my watch, and was astonished to see it was only ten to eleven. I really had been on the move—and wasn't even tired.

Call me Miss Lickety Split, I thought.

Marge was hovering near the kitchen entrance. "Can I get you something? Coffee or tea? I have some wafers a delightful young couple from Belgium left when—"

"I'm fine, Marge," I said. Though I suddenly wasn't. Just as I'd expected, my return to the Millwood had provoked a barrage of thoughts and feelings, and not just about the day I found Abe's body. My recollections of all the times we'd sat talking in this very room were equally strong, and in a certain way even more overwhelming. "On second thought," I said, hoping Marge hadn't noticed my emotional downturn, "maybe I could use a glass of cold water."

She went to get a pitcher from the fridge, giving me a chance to recover. I took a few deep breaths and was able to somewhat pull myself together by the time she returned.

"Well, now." Marge poured my water and then settled into a broad wingback chair opposite me.

"I'm happy to see you in a condition that isn't a dead faint."

"Thanks," I said. "I'm kind of glad not to be passed out drooling on your sofa."

Marge reached out and gave my knee a fond little slap. Old-time New Englanders aren't renowned for their sentimentality, and I'd gotten used to playing along with her arid humor.

"I should explain why I rushed you over here," she said, shifting her hefty backside in the chair. "As I always say, innkeeping is a 'ready' sort of profession. We need to set up quickly between bookings and move on from one to the next. Ready, ready, ready!"

I thought about that a second.

"So who're you getting ready for?" I asked.

"A very debonair gentleman," Marge said. "He's here on an overnight outing and has enjoyed Pigeon Cove so much he wants to come back next week for a longer stay."

I guessed that meant she wanted me to spiff up one of the guest rooms for him. But why had she insisted on discussing it in person?

Then it hit me.

"Marge," I said, "if you're asking what I think you are, I can't."

Marge gave me a look.

"At least consider it," she said. "The gentleman specifically requested my best and largest suite. And it has to be put in order at some point."

I remembered my first glimpse of the body, the blood on the carpet. And then I imagined what it would be like trying to get those horrible stains out of it.

"I can't," I said with a shudder. "I can't clean Abe's room."

Marge leaned forward.

"Did I tell you that awful yellow crime scene tape is still across its door?" she said. "The police have been clumping in and out. And not only Chief Vega and his officers. There've been detectives from Boston. Men in lab smocks. But they've finally said the tape can come down this weekend, and the room can't stay as it is right now."

"I understand," I said. "I'm just not the person you want doing the cleanup."

Marge shook her head in dismissal.

"You're the *only* person I want," she said. "The furnishings are irreplaceable. I can't trust anyone else not to damage them. I'd be willing to triple your usual pay, Sky."

I'd be dishonest if I claimed the money wasn't an enticement. Between Paul's medical bills and paying off the debt on his restaurant, our savings had been pretty well wiped out, and it would be sheer pleasure to have my wallet feel heavier than air for a change. Besides, three times Marge's generous usual was a lot—enough to pay off a credit card balance in one shot, and even help offset the expense of feeding Skiball, who'd proven to have an appetite as big as her mouth and was gobbling up cat food—and what little slack I'd gained in my budget since I started housecleaning—at a frightful rate.

Still, though, I wasn't sure I could handle it.

"There are a couple of other services on the Cape," I said. "I can get good recommendations . . ."

Marge gave me another look, holding her eyes steady on mine.

"If I have to use a different service, I'll understand, and try not to be too disappointed," she said. "But Mr. Monahan left his clothes in the room. A pile of old books that he'd bought on the way up from Florida and had been planning to drive over to that storage shed he leases from Rollie Evers. And a handful of other belongings. Say he could choose someone to ensure his things are put in order—anyone at all—who do you think it would be?"

That was easy. Especially when it came to the books, of course. It had been a mutual love of reading that sparked our friendship. I couldn't have counted how often Abe put on a whole elaborate show laying out the steals he'd gotten at some library or garage sale. For Abe, and maybe for both of us, it had seemed the highlight of his every visit to Pigeon Cove.

I felt that sorting and clearing out Abe's possessions would break my heart. But I was also thinking I probably shouldn't be worried about how it would make me feel. Thinking it might be important for friends to do such things for each other regardless.

I sat there across from Marge, trying to make up my mind. But I couldn't.

"Let me sleep on this before I decide, Marge," I said. "I'll have an answer in the morning. If I can't do the job, I promise I'll find you someone who will."

Marge nodded. I'd thought my tentativeness might make her impatient, but her gentle smile showed me I was wrong.

"That sounds fine," she said. "I won't force this on you. I won't even get angry and stop you from dusting, scrubbing, and polishing anything else you'd care to around here."

I was smiling too now. "Would that be at the usual rate?"

Marge's eyes were twinkling again.

"An offer of added pay is like lightning," she said. "It never strikes twice in the same spo—"

Marge was interrupted by the sound of the screen door opening and closing out back. A moment later her corgis started yapping and I heard a racket in the house behind me.

She raised her eyes, glancing over my shoulder toward the parlor's rear entryway.

"Here comes the young man I told you about!" she said.

"The one who wants to book Abe's room?"

Marge nodded, moved to the edge of her seat, and dropped her voice.

"He's such a handsome charmer," she said. "Wait, you'll see . . . He's with his uncle from Chicago today, so you can meet the two of them."

I blinked. It couldn't be . . . Could it?

"Does his uncle happen to have a dog?" I said.

"That's right. And she's the sweetest, most even-tempered creature—a rescued greyhound," Marge said. "My rotten babies did nothing but yap and snarl at her this morning, but she paid no attention to them whatsoever."

Before I could say another word, Marge stood up and waved to her guests. "Hello! Please come in!"

I turned partway around in my chair, and lo and behold. There in the entry were the pair I'd run into while jogging through Maplewood Park, the white-haired man and Rosie a step ahead of the guy in sunglasses.

"Hey, doll!" he said to me.

Marge looked surprised.

"You've met?" she said, looking around at me.

"Yep, in the park this morning," the white-haired man said. "Didn't get each other's monikers, though."

Marge seemed absolutely delighted by the coincidence—and the chance to make our introductions.

"Sky Taylor, meet Frank and Adam Kennedy— no relation to the Boston politicians, they insist!" she said, motioning from the older man to Sunglasses. "Frank and Adam, say hello to my friend Sky Taylor! Without her help, I could never maintain this inn."

The white-haired man—*Frank*—came over and offered me his right hand, holding Rosie's leash with the other.

"Fancy seein' you here!" he laughed. "Me, my

nephew, 'n Rosie really *must've* walked under a lucky star!"

"Actually, I think it's that shamrock I packed in my travel bag."

The second bit of pleasantry was from Sunglasses—Adam, that is. He'd taken off his sports wraps to reveal the palest blue eyes I'd ever seen and had a bright, open smile on his face that practically knocked me off my chair. Was this the same brusque character from the park?

"Seriously, I'm glad we've crossed paths again," he said, leaning forward to shake my hand. "It must be a sign of good things to come."

Marge clapped with excitement.

"There's no truer reward for an innkeeper than bringing people together from far and wide!" she said.

I'd forced a smile but hadn't said anything, mainly because I couldn't think of anything to say. Adam still had his hand around mine, and though I couldn't have explained why, I was very eager for him to let it go. Maybe it was the jarring personality transformation he seemed to have undergone since that morning, I don't know. But it put me off—and unlike in the park, I didn't feel my reaction was the slightest bit excessive. There was something about his newfound sociability that was a tad too fraudulent for my liking.

"Well, Adam, goes to show we were right to pick this hacienda," the white-haired man said. "You're gonna love it next week!"

Adam looked at him, nodded, and then turned

back in my direction. He was still radiating inexplicable cheerfulness.

"I definitely intend to make myself at home," he said. "Right here at the Millwood in Pigeon Cove."

I kept smiling but pulled my hand from his grasp, none too happy about that at all.

Chapter 8

"My good friends and loyal, steady customers . . . or even those of you who wound me by shopping in the supermarket's produce department . . . I must make a confession," said Gazi Del Turko, with a faint accent I'd heard was Turkish Italian. He had walked up to Abe's rock wall carrying a Freedom Bank canvas giveaway tote. "It is, you should know, a very big and serious confession about myself and Mister Abel."

The owner, manager, and sole employee of Del Turko's Tomatoes—a roadside stand that you hit just as you drive into town on Main Street—Gazi stood in front of Abe's rock wall looking sorrowful.

I think every one of the dozen or so people who'd turned up there in the lot shared Gazi's expression. I know that I did, in spite of the gushing morning sun, the pleasant scents of pine and earth around us, and our determination to make

the afternoon a celebration of Abe's life rather
than some grim, depressing memorial service.

The sadness was certainly evident on Chloe's
and Marge's faces. And Jessie Barton's. It was all
over Olivia Chase, the holistic veterinarian who'd
been Skiball's primary health-care provider since
Abe had been coming to town. I was convinced I
saw it on Bill Drecksel's face, which I admit I'd
been studying for signs of something more insidi-
ous. I even thought I saw it on Noel Lawless's
makeup-less and perpetually angry mug—though
considering that she was supposed to be the most
vocal of the Abe-haters, it kind of surprised me
that she'd showed up in the first place.

In all honesty, I was glad we weren't hiding
our blues. I'd been to several wakes where people
downed some fortifying drinks, put a clamp on
their grief, and took turns stepping up on a plat-
form to tell nothing but humorous stories about
someone who'd passed on. While I understood
that was just another way to mourn, and wasn't
the slightest bit judgmental about it, it wasn't
my way.

I mean, sure, most of us had funny memories
of Old Abe, and it definitely had been good hearing some of them that morning. Bertram the
shrimper, a grizzled, squint-eyed old salt who
hung around the Wing a lot, had spoken a few
words that drew smiles all around.

"Seein' him on the wharf with his readin' matter, I always asked Abe if he was up for the summer," Bert had said, thumbs thrust under his

suspenders, his thick beard wagging up and down
as he spoke. "That's how I'd say it, exact, if you're
curious. 'Up for the summer?' Exceptin' I'd ask
the same question whether the trees was in the
full green of June or we had autumn leaves or
winter snow coverin' the ground. Just to get a rise
out of him, y'know. 'Cause Abie fancied himself
a year-rounder, and didn't like bein' lumped in
with them summer folks that start a'moanin' and
a'shiverin' soon's the temperature hereabouts slips
a degree or two below seventy-five an' we're a
step closer to the shrimp harvest. So, every time,
it was 'Up for the summer?' to him. And, say it
was December or January, Abie would kinda
wrinkle that forehead of his, an' remind me what
season it was. But I'd keep a straight face, an-
swerin', 'Guess you got here early to open up
the house!' "

That one had actually made a few of us, including me, chuckle aloud. So had another recollection
from Oren Fipps, the realtor who'd brokered the
deal for Abe's lot years before. At the time, Oren
said, he'd been amazed at Abe's total ignorance
of what constituted an acre of land. "Please, talk
to me in feet and yards so I can understand you!"
Abe had insisted when considering his purchase.
"An acre . . . unless you're a farmer or a grazing
cow, who can picture an acre?"

Telling his story, Oren had demonstrated how
Mr. Monahan had thrown up his hands in frustra-
tion, an impression so right on I could almost see
Abe there in front of me.

There had been a few more anecdotes like that. And, again, I thought they were important and wonderful. But Abe was gone, and that was terribly sad, and we needed to let the sadness in too.

All this being said, Gazi had made me unexpectedly anxious and suspicious. Maybe it was because less than a day had passed since Jessie Barton clued me in about the town's sizable anti-Abe corps, but I wondered what he'd meant by the word "confession." And maybe, I thought, I was right to wonder. Abe hadn't just died; he'd been murdered—something I was certainly never going to forget.

The truth was I wanted to know who'd killed him. Wanted it desperately. And as I stood holding Skiball in the cat carrier my mom had FedExed for the occasion—she'd whipped it up out of fabric and foam padding practically overnight, stenciling the Japanese Kanji characters that stood for "New Beginnings" on the outside—I couldn't shake the thought that Gazi was about to drop a bombshell of remorse on us.

I glanced over at Chloe, who'd stuck close to my side amid the group gathered near the stone wall. She returned my look and began to slowly and soundlessly mouth something to me—but I couldn't quite read her lips and shook my head to let her know it.

Chloe's lips moved again. I still had no idea what she was trying to say, though.

"What?" I whispered.

"M-u-r-d-e-r-e-r," Chloe said in a low but audible voice, spelling out the word.

Which told me a couple of things. First, I wasn't alone in wondering what the tomato man was ready to confess. And second, I was starting to think way too much like my best friend the crime buff—a scary realization that I admit made me decide to check my own suspicions.

"Chloe, let's not jump to conclusions . . ."

"I read a novel where the fruit-and-vegetable man did it. His wife was having an affair with a hot-dog vendor, and he poisoned her tomatoes so they'd die eating salsa and chips in bed," she said, keeping her voice down to a hush. Then she jabbed her elbow into my rib cage, her head turning in Gazi's direction. "Here we go, dear. He's ready to spill his guts. You wait and see, he's brought the evidence in that freebie bag."

I looked up. After a long pause, Gazi had lowered his tote to the ground. A short man with a globelike head, oblong body, thick arms and legs, and bulbous toes sticking out of his brown leather sandals, he always looked to me like he'd been put together by a professional balloon twister.

Regarding everyone soberly, he said, "Since I was a little boy, I have loved tomatoes. When I came to this great country, this beautiful town, it was with a dream that I would open the greatest tomato stand in the world. And I have worked hard—very hard, my friends—to sell you only tomatoes of fine, fresh quality and delicious taste."

He cleared his throat. "I wish to thank many of you for your return business. I hope you will all keep coming as I expand my summer hours. But of all my many customers in Pigeon Cove, man or woman, it was Mister Abel who would most appreciate a truly good tomato—and that is why I must confess that he would receive discounts I would give no one else."

My eyes snapped to Chloe.

"So much for your confession theory," I said.

"*Shh,*" Chloe said. "It's a touching story anyway. And I'm curious about what's in the tote."

"Here is how I will remember Mister Abel," Gazi went on in an emotional tone. "I mean no offense to anyone here, but most of you do not know your tomatoes nearly well enough. For example, when you come shopping for beefsteak tomatoes, I must often ask which of the beefsteak varieties you mean, for not all are the same. Do you wish to purchase a pound of Bush Beefsteak? Beefmaster? Prime Beefsteak? Or perhaps the firm and meaty Pink Ponderosa? Dear customers, I cannot know unless you tell me. And while I do not believe any of you truly mean to waste my time, it does happen far too often—"

"So you're calling us tomato-ignorant, is that it?" Noel Lawless interrupted, thrusting her chin out at Gazi. "Because if you are, I'm taking issue."

A murmur of surprise ran through our little group. Everybody knew Noel was on a perpetual hair trigger. But I guess none of us had expected her to start firing hostile volleys at our ceremony . . . though I must admit Gazi's remarks left me feeling sort of insulted too.

And then it struck me—given the hotter-than-a-matchstick head perched on Noel's combative shoulders, was it totally out of the question that *she'd* killed Abe? I mean, it seemed insane to think his offer to help her down some slippery porch steps could have brought about a lasting resentment, let alone one so strong it would fuel a murderous rage several months later. But since when was murder ever sane behavior?

Before I had a chance to contemplate it—or listen to Noel launch into a militant tirade—Gazi offered her an even, forbearing smile.

"I call no one ignorant, Ms. Noel," he said. "Rather, I am calling Mister Abel tomato-*wise*. A gentleman who knew the subtle differences between the many beefsteaks. Who never would simply ask for plum tomatoes, but tell me whether he wanted Novas, Napolis, or Romas. A gentleman who, I would add, made tomato sauce, tomato paste, and catsup from my dear wife Cemile's recipe booklet, available free at my stand with every purchase of twenty-five dollars and over."

For whatever reason, that explanation did the trick. As Noel appeared to settle down and Gazi bent to unzip his Freedom Bank tote, I was thinking, apropos of nothing, that he was obviously a person who not only liked accepting giveaways but also liked giving them away.

Beside me, meanwhile, Chloe rose up on her toes to get an advance peek at whatever he'd brought in the bag.

I already figured I knew—and I was right.

Gingerly, one by one, Gazi pulled about a half dozen tomatoes out of it and set them in a row atop the rock wall. There was a big fat orange tomato, a medium round tomato, and a small red pear-shaped tomato. There was a yellow tomato, a green tomato, and even an absolutely white tomato. I admit I didn't know the varieties by name. Funny, though, I was absolutely certain Paul would have. Just as Old Abe had known. My husband and my friend, both gone now with something they'd shared without ever having met—and that I suddenly regretted not having learned from them while they were here.

It was a small thing, sure. But I've found out those small things do add up. At our very best with each other, I believe we neglect so much.

I squeezed the handle of Skiball's carrier tightly, lowered my head, and looked at her through the mesh front panel.

"Love you, little girl," I said softly.

"Mik-kee-ee," she replied, pushing a paw against my nose through the mesh.

"Mister Abel, I leave these here for you," Gazi was saying over by the wall. His voice cracked. "They are perfect specimens, ripened to the fullest in the best of local greenhouses, picked by my own hand from among the wholesaler's many bushels. May your soul find the sweetness locked within them . . . Good-bye.''

'With that, Gazi lifted his empty tote off the ground and rejoined the rest of us. I heard sniffles around me, saw Chloe dab her eyes with a handkerchief. I thought even Noel looked momentarily subdued, but maybe that was my imagination.

Then Marge Millwood was at the wall offering her own recollections. She spoke mainly about what an ideal guest he'd been at her inn, and it was nice, and true to who Abe had been. Always kept his bookings and arrived on schedule, she said. Not once had she heard a fuss out of him. An insightful and receptive conversationalist with Marge and her other guests, able to hold his own on any subject. Never wasteful—he didn't fill his breakfast dish with more than he could eat from the buffet, so that Marge would have to throw the leftover food in the trash. Courteous, considerate, and outstandingly *clean* . . .

"Let me tell you—and Sky Taylor can back me on this—Abel Monahan was the kind of man who wouldn't think of leaving a mess around for somebody else to pick up. I'd walk into his room after he'd checked out, and it was just like he'd never been there. The bed made. The pillows fluffed. He'd run a damp cloth over the furniture to get rid of cat hair and dander, give the bathtub a once-over with a sponge and cleanser, and even scrub the toilet with that brush I keep alongside it. When I'd go inspect the soap dish, I'd know I wouldn't see a trace of scum." Marge paused and took a breath. "One, two, sometimes as many as four hours a day, Abel would come here to work on this wall, but not a single time did he come back to the Millwood and track dirt across the carpets or wood floors.

"As most of you know, running an inn isn't only my pride and joy, it's in my blood. My mother did it, and my grandmother too. Which makes me a third-generation innkeeper for those of you who can't count—and yes that's a joke, so feel free to allow yourselves a smile. But I'm not joking, or spouting hot air, when I tell you that if I could have wished for the guest of my dreams, ordered him cooked right up from scratch out of God's oven, it would have been Abel Monahan. That's the highest compliment I can pay a man. And that's all I've got to say—except have a pleasant day and thank you folks for coming to our send-off."

After Marge was finished, we heard a string of brief testimonials from some of Abe's more peripheral friends and acquaintances. Beverly Boatman, president of the Pigeon Cove Historical Society, expressed her regard for Abe's knowledge of the past. Grace Blossom the horticulturist—no, I've never believed for a minute that's her real surname—talked about his love and appreciation of growing things. Steve Drake of the Architectural Preservation Committee also had some starched but admiring words.

And then, as Steve began wrapping up, a loud, hitching sob from over to my right suddenly drew everyone's attention. Our heads all turned in that direction as Bill Drecksel went shoving up to the wall, bumping into Noel Lawless and almost bowling her over in the process.

"Hey, you big moose, watch where you put your hands," she said angrily.

Drecksel ignored her. I realized he had tears his eyes and that they must have been blinding him, because he kind of shambled over to the wall, almost tripping over Steve Drake's feet as he pushed him aside.

"I can't listen to you talk about those old buildings another second!" Drecksel wailed. "I've got to get something off my chest right now!"

I tried not to glance around at Chloe this time, but she kept elbow-jabbing me until I relented.

As I'd expected, she was mouthing the letters of that word again. "M-u-r-d . . ."

I looked away, fixing my attention on Drecksel. He'd turned his back to the rest of us, put his hands on top of the wall, and started rocking up and down over it while continuing to sob uncontainably.

"Why did we have to fight, Abe? *Why?*" he howled loud enough to scare some birds up from a nearby tree. "This wall . . . look at it, it's built around nothing. *Nothing!* I tell you I'll pay top dollar for this land, and you won't take it. I tell you I'll throw in a stupendous condo in Getaway

Groves—its ritziest building—and you turn me down flat! And for what? Rocks! Rocks! A pile of ugly, stupid rocks!"

Marge had hastily stepped close to him.

"Bill Drecksel, you should be ashamed of yourself for this outburst—"

He spun around, and I could see the tears running down his cheeks in rivulets.

"No! I got to say what I got to say," he exclaimed and pushed the balls of his palms into his temples. "Abe Monahan was a good guy! A *great* guy! Ten years we're friends. A whole decade! But when I make him an offer that'll set him up pretty, he's got to be stubborn and hang on to a useless dirt lot! And so we fight and scream at each other, and I yell something I shouldn't've yelled, and I never get a chance to tell him I'm sorry." Drecksel's eyes turned skyward, his hands flying off his bald head and waving high in the air. "Maybe it's too late, Abe, but here you go anyway! I should've kept my stupid mouth shut! I never wanted you to leave town! I'm sorry I cursed at you! I'm sorry, I'm sorry, I'm sorry—"

I'm positive Drecksel would've crumpled to his knees if Jessie Barton hadn't come rushing over to him at that moment, throwing her arms around his burly chest. Instead, he returned her hug and buried his face against her shoulder, dissolving into another spate of inconsolable sobs.

It took a few minutes for everything to get settled. Jessie, who'd given Drecksel a lift over in her car, walked him back to it, reappeared long enough to let us know she was driving him home, and then left. I guess that was when I knew I felt sorry for Bill, and found myself moving him lower down on my list of murder suspects. It was possible, I suppose, that his hysteria had been some sort of performance. But I didn't believe he was that skilled an actor. And who would he have been putting on a show for? As far as Bill was concerned, Jessie was the only one at the ceremony who knew of his squabble with Abe. There had been no reason for him to throw a public fit, no way it could have done anything but open him up to scrutiny.

I didn't have much time to think about it, though. As soon as Jessie and Drecksel had gone, I'd taken a head count of everyone in the lot, and it confirmed what I'd probably known in the first place—my turn at the wall had come around.

Mine and Skiball's.

I pulled in a deep breath and carried her over to it, reviewing all the Abe stories that were in my head, trying to choose which of them to tell. Really, I had so many . . . I'd thought of a dozen the night before, maybe more. There was the time I took Abe on a whale-watching cruise and saw a mother breach with her calf. There was the afternoon we drove down to Salem and visited the Turner-Ingersoll Mansion, which had inspired Hawthorne to write *The House of the Seven Gables*— Abe had educated me about its history and the legends surrounding it, and pointed out all its elaborate architectural touches. Afterward we'd gone to the site of a witch trial, and through the Peabody Museum, and then taken a walk along the harbor, where the tall ships had once anchored and women had gathered to wait for their seafaring men to come home from distant journeys.

As I stood at the wall, my memories of Abe rose up to swamp me. So many memories, I found myself unable to decide which of them to contribute to the ceremony.

And maybe that was for the best, because I think I'd have gotten too choked up to get any of them out.

Holding Skiball, then, I turned to the crowd and thought about the most important thing I could add on behalf of both of us. I only hoped it would be enough.

"Abel Monahan was our friend," I said. "We'll remember him as long as memory remains."

Chapter 9

At eight o'clock on Friday night, Mike Ennis and I were out having dinner at Linaria, a Greek seafood restaurant in a two-story redbrick building on Rogers Street opposite the working docks of Gloucester's Inner Harbor. Mike had picked me up at the Fog Bell in his Mini Cooper, which was sort of cramped if you were a human being of average proportions but would probably be the ideal size for Skiball's first set of wheels when she was old enough to qualify for her driver's license. Just so long as she didn't try squeezing any of her huskier feline friends into the backseat.

As Mike had promised, the atmosphere at Linaria was Old World friendly. Each of the dozen or so tables had a white tablecloth and napkins and a ceramic vase of fresh, tastefully arranged flowers. Most were set for no more than two to four diners. The restaurant's small capacity, carpeted floor, and stone fireplace with a crackling blaze gave it a warm, intimate coziness. According to Mike, it was one of the few places around where you could have a quiet conversation even when there was a full house.

Mike had mentioned that, and a bunch of other things about Linaria, at our table while we were waiting to be served. He told me it was named after a tiny island in western Greece that had been the ancestral home of its owners, who'd immigrated to America several generations ago. He had told me the owners' son and his wife, Alex and Ruthie, were the ones mainly running the show nowadays, and that both had solid culinary pedigrees. The eldest of three brothers, Alex had practically grown up in the restaurant during its early years, when his family hadn't been able to afford a babysitter, and he'd hung around every day after school, helping out with this and that once he finished his homework. As a result, there was nothing about the business he didn't know or couldn't do, nor any dish on the menu he wasn't able to prepare. Very much likewise, Ruthie, a top-notch baker and pastry chef, had spent a big chunk of *her* childhood in her parents' Boston bakery. Together they'd built upon and diversified the appeal of what had already been Cape Ann's oldest established eating spot.

I suppose I ought to explain that Mike knew all this because the restaurant's owners were his paternal grandparents and because Alex Elpidios was his favorite uncle—both of which were tidbits he had neglected to share in advance. Instead I'd found out for myself when Alex showed up to welcome him at the door.

"All right, here you are!" Uncle Alex had said, his bearish embrace squeezing the wind out of Mike. He gave him a loud, smacking kiss on the cheek, glanced at me, and smiled. "Hello, young lady! Mama said our nephew was bringing a friend!"

Which put Uncle Alex at least a step up on me, I'd thought. To be fair, Mike had mentioned being close to the people who ran the place. But "close" could have meant they were friends. Or simply that he was a regular. And while I supposed it might have been construed as a warning that I'd be meeting the family, I wouldn't have minded being a little better prepared for it.

"Sky—what a beautiful name!" Uncle Alex had said as Mike gasped out introductions between hugs. *"He'ro poli!"*

I'd smiled politely.

"Excuse me?"

Uncle Alex had seemed puzzled. He was a big, olive-complected man in his sixties wearing a well-tailored pin-striped suit, a white monogrammed shirt, glossy tasseled loafers, and a platinum Rolex wristwatch that must have cost a fortune.

"Come on," he said, "I *know* you speak Greek!"

"Actually," I said, "I don't."

"But your background's Greek, no?"

I shook my head.

"No," I said, "it isn't."

"I don't believe it! How can you not be Greek?" Uncle Alex was still giving Mike effusively affectionate chest compressions. "Look at you! That black hair! Those brown eyes! How's it possible?"

I shrugged.

"It happens, I guess."

Uncle Alex frowned and released Mike from his clutches.

"She's a kidder, right? *Tell* me she's Greek."

"I never asked," Mike said, catching his breath. "But if she says she isn't, she isn't, and that's all there is to it." He paused to tuck in his shirt and straighten his ruffled tie and sport jacket. *"He'ro poli* means 'nice to meet you,' by the way."

"Oh," I said.

"In Greek, that is."

"I sort of assumed," I said. "But thanks for clarifying."

"Stop pulling my leg, you two!" Uncle Alex sounded beleaguered. "What'll happen when I'm old and senile? You going to try telling me I'*m* not Greek?" He faced me again. "Skyros," he said with a meaningful look.

"What?"

"Skyros," he repeated. "That's your full name. After the harbor in the middle of Linaria. It's the birthplace of my parents *and* the name of this restaurant." He put a hand on my arm, guiding me gently out of the way as a couple of diners came through the entrance. "Your parents name you Skyros like the harbor, they're Greek. No ifs, ands, or buts."

I shrugged again.

"Maybe so," I said. "But my name isn't Skyros like the harbor. It's Sky, like the blue sky. Which is what my mother and father had in mind when they gave it to me, don't ask."

Uncle Alex had stood there looking at me.

"You really shouldn't fight me on this, it breaks my heart," he said, pounding his chest with a fist for emphasis. "Well, it's busy around here. I'd better go take care of some things. See you later!"

Uncle Alex gave the new arrivals a hospitable smile, turned us over to a perky blond hostess, and then rushed off through a doorless entry near the bar. Beyond it, I glimpsed a descending staircase against an exposed brick wall.

As Uncle Alex plunged downstairs, Mike and I fell into step behind the hostess.

Our table was by the fireplace, about halfway toward the rear. She showed us over to it, handed us our menus, and left us alone.

"Okay," I said, looking across at Mike. "How do I answer your uncle the next time he snap quizzes my Greek comprehension?"

"Well," he said, "I suppose 'I still don't understand' would work okay."

I smiled.

"I know that sort of thing can be awkward," Mike said. "Sorry you had to put up with it."

"No big deal," I said with a shrug. "Your uncle seems like a real sweetheart."

Mike opened his menu on the table, slipped an eyeglass case from his inner jacket pocket, and sort of fidgeted with it.

"It isn't so much him," he said, shaking his head. "I could've sworn that I'd mentioned the restaurant belonged to members of my family. But I guess I didn't, huh?"

I gave him a look.

"No," I said. "You most definitely did not."

Mike fiddled around with the case for a minute, took out a pair of wire-rimmed reading glasses.

"You know, my family name is Elpidios, same as Uncle Alex's," he said, wiping his lenses with a cleaning cloth. "Ennis is its anglicized form . . . It's an easier byline to remember."

I couldn't resist. "The way Sky might be easier to remember than Skyros," I said. "If that was my name."

Mike cleared his throat, rubbing his glasses so hard you would have thought he'd picked them up out of a mud puddle. He looked embarrassed, and I instantly regretted my little quip.

"I could use some pointers on what to order," I said, thinking a change of subject might be prudent. "Pick out something yummy and all's well."

Mike smiled.

"Instant atonement, I can dig it," he said. "Give me a sec."

He inspected his glasses, gave them a final touchup, decided they were good to go, and had no sooner slipped them on than one of the lenses popped out, twirling over in the air once or twice to catch the firelight before landing on the table.

Whoops.

Have you ever had one of those times when

you get an inkling that even the simplest things are going to be . . . well, not so simple?

I didn't laugh. I admit I felt the urge, but I didn't. Mike seemed flustered, looking at me through his half-empty frames. And I wanted to avoid having my night out become one of those unsimple occasions.

He removed his glasses and examined them. The screw that held the left side of the frame together had slipped out, causing the frame to come apart at the endpiece. Hence, the lens doing its impression of a Flying Wallenda.

"I can't believe this," he said.

"Did you see where the screw fell?" I asked.

Mike shook his head. He looked on top of the table but didn't find it. He lifted his napkin to see if the screw had rolled under it, didn't find it there either. He searched for it on the carpet on either side of his chair, feeling around in case it had slipped into the nap. When that proved fruitless, he took one last shot, bent forward, and peered under the table.

Pay dirt. He reached out and came up with it. I can't say he looked much happier than before, though.

"No way I can put this back in," he said, holding the tiny screw between his thumb and forefinger. "Not without one of those little screwdrivers."

What did I tell you? Simple, not so simple. These things have a way of mounting.

Still, you've got try and stem the tide.

"Hang on," I said. "I might be able to help."

I stood up, went over to the bar, and got a wooden toothpick from the dispenser. It was the thin, tapered kind, which was perfect.

I returned to the table and asked Mike for his frame and lens. Then I set the lens back in place, pressed the frame together around it with the top and bottom halves of the endpiece aligned, and inserted the narrow end of the toothpick into the vacant screw hole. Finally I snapped off the top of the toothpick and put it aside.

When I let go of the frame, the lens stayed right where it belonged.

"Here," I said, handing Mike's glasses back to him. "It's a temporary fix, but it'll hold if you're careful."

Mike looked at me, put the glasses on his face, and smiled.

"This is ingenious, Sky," he said. "A *toothpick*."

I shrugged.

"What can I tell you—I'm versatile," I said and pointed to my menu. "Now that you can read this thing, you'd better let me know what's good before another calamity strikes."

He did. I ordered mackerel with seasoned tomato sauce, and Mike ordered a mysterious dish called *bourtheto*, and we both took the waiter's suggestion and ordered the house-specialty carrot bisque as our appetizer. Last, we asked for a carafe of Vermont Chardonnay off the wine list.

Then we talked for a while. I found out about Linaria's origins, and Alex and Ruthie, and the rest.

It was just as I'd noticed the waiter approaching with our carafe that I saw Uncle Alex reemerge from the doorway near the bar, a wine bucket in his hands. Heading off the waiter, he waved him aside and swiftly carried the bucket to our table.

"Do I have to show you kids how to live it up?" he said. "That local wine's fine for a regular occasion, but this white Kourtaki's from my exclusive stock."

Mike looked at me, his reading glasses off.

"My uncle is very proud of his wine cellar," he said.

"The *best* wine cellar on the north coast," Uncle Alex amplified. He wrapped a napkin around the bottle, lifted it from its bed of ice, and pulled the cork. "You'll love this, trust me. It's imported from Greece." He gave me a wink. "The vineyards are in Evia—could be you know about it, Sky. It's right there on the Mediterranean coast."

Mike sighed. "Uncle Alex, she already told you she isn't—"

"Okay, forget it, people are entitled to reveal what they want about themselves. Who knows, maybe she's hiding out from someone!" He laughed and filled our glasses. "Lots of people come to Cape Ann to hide, right Mr. Hotshot Crime Reporter?"

"Uncle Alex—"

"Just kidding. I'm off again, enjoy!" Uncle Alex poked my shoulder, his eyes gleaming. "Don't forget to eat Ruthie's sourdough bread with your carrot soup—it can't be beat!"

And with that he set the bottle back in the bucket and hustled away.

Now I looked at Mike, saw that he was holding up his wineglass, and raised mine off the table.

"To Greece," he said with a wry grin.

"And the grapes of Evia-by-the-Sea," I said.

We clinked glasses, sipped.

"I should've expected my uncle to keep tabs on our orders," Mike said.

I smiled. "He means well. And the wine's delicious."

Mike had settled into his chair, visibly relaxed. "It is, isn't it?" he said.

I nodded again, and we talked some more, and then the waiter brought our carrot soups and a large basket of the homemade bread.

The combination lived up to Uncle Alex's hearty endorsement.

"Dill seeds," I said, tasting the soup. "Pretty exceptional."

Mike gave me an inquisitive look.

"You'll find a lot of carrot soups seasoned with dill leaves," I explained. "But it's rare for the cook to use ground seeds."

Mike seemed surprised. "One spoonful and you can tell the difference?"

I nodded.

"The seeds give it more of a tang," I said. "I should know. My husband used to own a restaurant that specialized in soups. It was called the Souper Bowl. That's spelled S-o-u-p-e-r."

Mike chuckled.

"Clever," he said.

"The name was my biggest contribution," I said, and paused. I'd seen Mike glance briefly at my wedding band. "Paul died about two years ago. He'd been very ill, but I guess you'd say it was still unexpected. I kind of take it for granted that everybody at the office knows my story . . . the Digger's forte being the unearthing and dissemination of gossip."

Mike nodded. He had an understanding smile on his face.

"I'd heard," he said. "It must have been rough."

I took a drink and sat reflecting a moment. The wine was warm going down my throat.

"They say it's proper etiquette for a widow to put her wedding ring on her right hand instead of her left, but I'm not there yet, I guess," I said, surprised to find myself mentioning that to Mike. As things would have it, though, the sudden realization that I was comfortable with the subject made me just as suddenly shy away from it. "Anyway, Paul was a tremendous chef—he'd graduated from the Culinary Institute, worked at a bunch of four-star restaurants, and always wanted a place of his own. So we invested a chunk of our savings and took out a start-up loan. Our place was in Manhattan—a small bistro on the Lower West Side."

"Did you help him run it?"

I shook my head.

"We agreed that one of us needed to bring home a weekly paycheck. You know, keep a financial floor under us while the restaurant was getting established. Besides, I liked my job."

"Which was?"

"I wrote for an advertising agency," I said, and took another drink. "Ever see those television commercials with the Ridley Resorts snowbird? When he flutters down onto somebody's shoulders and whispers enticements to travel in his ears?"

"Sure. And the next thing the guy's hanging out with the bird in Cancún or South Beach, and they're wearing shades and sipping drinks poolside," Mike said. " 'Come chill where it's warm, baby!' "

I nodded.

"That's my line," I said. "In fact, it was my idea to have the bird make our pitch. Earlier on he had a human partner who did the talking."

Mike grinned. "I always got a kick out of that one."

"Everybody did. The campaign was a smash," I said. "Afterward, an Australian airline asked us for a knockoff of the character that would play overseas. So I cooked up the Bungee Budgie . . . instead of flying out of the sun, he'd come swinging down from a branch on a bungee cord."

"How'd that one do?"

"Pretty well," I said. "Honestly, I wasn't too fond of the budgie. His Aussie accent was cute, but it was like he was riding high on another bird's tailfeathers."

Mike laughed.

"The shameless pecker," he said.

We were quiet for a while, eating our soup and drinking our wine.

"So," Mike said, "how'd you wind up living in Pigeon Cove?"

"I'm not sure I know where to start," I said. "Well, not true. I do. But it's sort of a long story."

Mike took the wine bottle from the ice bucket and refilled our glasses.

"I'm in no rush," he said.

I drank, nodded.

"Paul and I just sort of stumbled onto the Cove," I said. "When you've got a restaurant, you have to keep an eye on it. Ask Uncle Alex, I'm sure he'd tell you. There's always too much happening to leave things to your staff. But the Souper Bowl was closed Sundays, and sometimes when business hit the doldrums—say, on a Saturday in July or August—Paul would leave his staff to look after things for the day, and we'd hop in the car and take off for the weekend. It was always spur of the moment." I paused. "One of those trips was a drive up the New England coast, and we needed a place to stay overnight, and found the Fog Bell. Chloe Edwards and I instantly hit it off and became tight friends. She's got such a big heart . . . When I lost Paul, she invited me to stay at the inn till I pulled myself together, and I decided to take her up on it." I reached for my glass again. "Chloe refused to charge for room and board, but I had to repay her kindness somehow. That's really how my cleaning service got its start."

"You offered to help out around the inn?"

I nodded.

"I'm inclined toward that sort of thing. Housekeeping, minor repairs—"

"Fixing eyeglasses . . ."

I smiled.

"That too," I said, and had a deep swallow of wine. "It's nice having Chloe's companionship. But I'm hoping to eventually buy a place, maybe one of those shingle cottages near the water, and need to get a financial leg up." I shrugged. "When I realized my knack could be marketable in a town full of grand old homes and understaffed inns, I was in business."

Mike was looking at me with his dark, perceptive eyes. The firewood in the hearth popped and snapped.

"I admire how you've handled things," he said. "You're a very resourceful person."

"Oh, I don't know. Like the saying goes, necessity's a mother. Or something like that."

Mike shook his head.

"Not everyone adapts," he said. "Some people can't or won't find their footing."

I didn't say anything. I felt slightly flushed with wine and was content to let our conversation breathe, enjoy Mike's attentiveness, and finish the carrot bisque.

The waiter brought our dinners. My mackerel fillet was delectable, but I have to admit Mike's *bourtheto* was scary. Served right in the baking pan, it looked like it consisted of an entire massacred school of fish. Small, plump, silvery ones, with their heads lopped off and the rest of their bodies intact . . . skin, fins, and all. The dish smelled appetizing enough—there was some peppery-garlicky thing going on with the light red sauce stirred into the pan—but that jumbled mass of decapitated fish bodies negated the aromatic appeal for me.

"Care to try some of this?" Mike asked, his serving spoon buried in the headless heap. "It's great."

I wanted to look worldly. I think I barely managed to avoid shuddering.

"No thanks," I said. "My portion's about all I can handle."

"Well, there's plenty here if you change your mind." Mike speared a fish and chewed it whole. "Most restaurants use chunks of cod or snapper in this dish instead of sprat, which is what these little guys are called . . . they're related to herring. It's almost impossible to find *bourtheto* prepared the traditional way in this country."

"Imagine that," I said.

Mike swallowed, nodded. "Go to other parts of the world, sprat is an expensive delicacy. It's usually canned and served in oil. But until a handful of years ago, when foreign countries passed strict regulations to stop the practice, American fisherman in their waters *discarded* them."

"What a waste," I said, thinking they'd tossed at least one panful too few from their nets.

Mike was nodding again.

"There's a Dutch factory trawler that sits outside the harbor sometimes—you've probably seen it from the waterfront. One of those megaships. My uncle cut a deal with the owners to sell him sprat they usually process for export markets. They charge him a premium, but I figure it's worth it for the authentic taste."

"Totally worth it, I'm sure," I said, and wondered why Uncle Alex wouldn't just save a few dollars picking up his ingredients at a local bait-and-tackle shop.

A moment later I decided to initiate Subject Change Number Two. It was either that or bite my tongue the next time Mike raved about his dish, which would have made chewing my food very painful.

"The *Anchor* must be quite a switch for you," I said. "After writing for a big-time newspaper, I mean."

Mike looked thoughtful.

"It's different," he said. "You pound a crime beat in DC, follow squad cars and ambulance sirens to the worst of scenes, it's hard not to burn out. At least it was for me." He hesitated. "I don't know. Maybe I'm just not made for city life and wanted an excuse to come back home."

I took a long drink of wine and felt it working on me.

"When I think about what happened to my friend Old Abe . . . Abel Monahan, that is"—I paused to figure out what I was trying to say—"I suppose the last thing you expected to cover right here in Pigeon Cove was a murder."

Mike sighed.

"Yes and no," he said. "We all live in one world, and the Cove's part of it. We sometimes feel like it isn't, I guess. And with reason. It's one of the nicer, quieter places you'll find. But it's not perfect. Everyplace under the sun and moon is connected to every other place . . . and those connections run through people with the same basic emotions and desires." His gaze found mine. "That's a lesson I learned in Washington, Sky. When there's world and want, bad things can happen."

I was quiet. I got the feeling Mike had shared something he ordinarily didn't. Maybe even shared more than was apparent on the surface.

In hindsight, that's probably what made me decide to tell him about the dilemma I'd been grappling with since my stop at Marge's earlier that day.

"Marge Millwood—she runs the inn where Mr. Monahan was killed, of course—Marge has asked me to clean out Abe's room," I said. "The police investigators are through with it, and it's okay to open it up again, and she's got someone who wants to book it next week."

Mike had been listening with interest. "What'd you tell her?"

"That I need to think about it overnight. She was very generous with her offer, and the money would come in handy. But I'm not sure about going through Abe's personal effects." Not to mention cleaning away his bloodstains, I thought but didn't say. It wasn't somewhere I wanted my mind to linger.

Mike put down his fork and sat forward.

"I can see how hard it would be," he said. "On the other hand, it's got to be done. And you have to consider who Abel would trust to do it right."

I nodded.

"Marge made the same point," I said. "It's the main reason I haven't turned her down yet."

"But . . . ?"

"I'm not sure I'm up to it. Nothing more complicated, really."

Mike looked at me.

"If you do decide you're able, I'll tag along and keep you company."

I smiled. "I appreciate the offer, but it isn't necessary," I said. "I just don't know that it would make things any easier."

Mike was shaking his head.

"I think I need to explain," he said, and hesitated. "Sky, I hope this doesn't sound cold, but it would be a help to me."

I drew up straight, my wineglass simultaneously sinking from my lips.

"A help?"

"Right," Mike said.

"To *you*?"

Mike nodded, leaned slightly forward.

"A couple of days ago I tried to get into the

room for a look around—you can do that sometimes as a member of the press, even while it's
still taped off. Vega was willing to oblige. I've got
a great relationship with him, but the detectives
from Boston red-lighted me without explanation."
He paused for a moment. "I've already asked
Marge Millwood to give me a peek at the things
Abel left behind, and she refused outright. Said it
would be inappropriate. But it occurs to me she
might not have any objection if you and I went in
there together."

I stared at Mike for about thirty seconds, wanting to believe I'd somehow misunderstood him,
but knowing I hadn't. I felt foolish. Utterly foolish.
First I'd gone and opened up to him—okay, an
understandable slip. I'd been enjoying his company, and my dinner, and just having a night out
for a change. I couldn't beat myself over the head
for that. But I was a grown, experienced woman,
not a schoolgirl. How could I have been gullible
enough to confuse his opportunism for consider-
ation?

Mike looked at me. His face said he'd recognized his mistake. Or recognized he'd made one—
I wouldn't have bet anything that he knew what
it was.

"Sky, what's wrong?" he said, bearing out my
suspicion.

I sat there speechless. The soft buzz I'd gotten
from the wine had abruptly become a knot of
tightness in my forehead. I wondered about Mike's
reason for asking me out. He couldn't have known

about Marge's proposition that day at the *Anchor*.
She hadn't even made it at the time, so that
wouldn't have been his motive. But he'd known
about me and Abe. Known I was neck-deep in the
murder investigation. It had been all over the
Cove, all over the office. Was charming information out of me on his mind when he'd toted Skiball over from the copy room? Could that have
been his intention from the start?

It would have been simple to believe it of him,
maybe as simple to dismiss it.

Instead, I unsimply continued to wonder.

A few more minutes passed in brittle silence.
Neither of us ate what was left on our plates, and
I even saw some dead fish stranded in Mike's pan.
The busboy came to clear the table, and the waiter
returned with a pair of dessert menus. He recom-
mended Ruthie's halva and baklava rolls if we
wanted Greek, and then went over some standard
sweets—cream puffs, chocolate or apple pie.

I was glad Uncle Alex didn't show up with his
own suggestions. He'd gone out of his way to
make me welcome and didn't deserve to have his
feelings hurt.

The waiter waited. Mike and I sat there staring
at each other over our menus.

"Sky?" he said uneasily. "Care for anything?"

I shook my head without a peep and handed
my menu back to the waiter.

Mike looked up at him, did the same.

"I think you'd better bring us the check," he said.

Chapter 10

I awoke Saturday feeling crystal clear about my answer to Marge Millwood. Sometimes it's like that when I have to make a hard decision. I'll move it to a mental back burner and let it simmer. If I'm lucky, everything comes together while I sleep.

Because it was too early to phone Marge—Skiball had proved to be the world's most irritating alarm clock, jumping up on my bed first thing every morning to use it as a kitty gym, with my chest substituting for a trampoline and my outstretched legs providing a convenient running track—I took a shower, had a cup of coffee, and went out to water Chloe's garden to kill an hour or so. When I came back upstairs, I found a phone message from Mike Ennis on my machine. He apologized for calling so early, but said he'd been up all night thinking about what happened at the restaurant and asked me to get back to him when I had a chance.

I didn't know whether I would. I wasn't sure I was ready to talk, or that it could lead to anything but more tension between us. Besides, he could say whatever he wanted to me when we inevitably ran into each other at the *Anchor*. I had other concerns in the meantime.

Getting in touch with Marge was right up top. I could barely wait to phone her, knowing it would lift a major weight off my shoulders.

I called her at nine o'clock and was at the Millwood Inn before ten, carrying my bag of tricks upstairs to Abe's room.

As it happened, cleaning it out wasn't the grimly painful experience I'd feared it would be. On the contrary, I believe it gave me a certain comfort that I might not have felt otherwise. Handling Abe's things, especially the books he'd loved, somehow put me in touch with him one last time and let me say good-bye as best I could have.

The same could even be said for my most unpleasant task—removing the dried reddish-brown stains from the rug and the bedclothes. Trite as it may sound, it's easy to say you're a friend in the good times, the times when it doesn't involve strength and sacrifice. But we all have to face our dark times, and we can only hope there's someone who will stand with us when they come—and take care of whatever we're unable to do for ourselves. Abe was gone. He'd had to face his darkest moment without a friend at his side. I'd had no chance to be there for him then. But I was here now to take care of anything I could for him, and finish what he'd left undone as he might have wished.

I also have to admit to something else. Remember when I said I enjoyed figuring stuff out that other people couldn't? I mentioned it while explaining that I'd identified with Abe's pleasure in finding different-sized rocks for his wall—a lot of them having emerged from soil he'd turned up planting his tomatoes and peppers, others gathered from beaches where they'd lain unnoticed for heaven knows how long, in plain view of anyone inclined to look and see them. And I mean *really* see them. Not only for what they were separately, but for how they could all be put together as a whole.

Well, I had a little of that same feeling—maybe even more than just a little—as I went through Abe's possessions one at a time. I think I was hoping to find some clue, or clues, among them about who'd taken his life. I think I felt I'd be the one who could recognize them if they were there. I think I knew the lure of the puzzle and the satisfaction I would get from solving it. And I also think Old Abe would have understood completely.

Anyway, it was late afternoon before I'd gotten the room in shape and, with an assist from Marge, carried the last of Abe's belongings down to my Toyota. There wasn't really that much. A single wheeled suitcase full of clothes, one of those hanging toiletry bags, and twenty or thirty hardbound books that he'd neatly organized and stacked by category.

Before we brought the stuff out, Marge suggested that I phone Rollie Evers, the guy who owned the storehouse where Abe rented a space for stashing and packing his treasured book finds, and ask if he'd be okay with me bringing over the final batch, along with Abe's luggage. I thought it was a sensible idea. I'd met Evers more than once while helping Abe haul books over, so he knew who I was, and might not have a problem with letting me inside. Abe had kept all sorts of mailing items in the unit, which was about the size of a walk-in closet. I figured I could box up the books in sturdy cartons and see if he'd prepared any other packages to be shipped. And who knew, maybe I'd find one addressed to a friend or family member who might want to claim his possessions.

"It ain't my policy, but Monahan was an okay duffer," Evers told me over the phone in Marge's parlor. "You hurry, I'll open up the room. Except I can't stick around later'n six o'clock. My wife's draggin' me out to that 'plex down in Salem, and the flick starts at seven."

I glanced at my watch. It was almost five, and we hadn't even loaded up the SUV yet.

"That's going to be tight," I said. "Does tomorrow morning work any better?"

Evers produced a phlegmy, grumbling sound. "I ain't never here on Sundays," he said. "The Good Book says that's when I got to stay home on my Lay-Z-Boy."

"Look, I'll leave as soon as possible," I said. "The most I'd be is five, ten minutes late. If even that—"

"You want to pay for my night out?"

"I'm not sure I understand . . ."

"I asked if you got thirty bucks to cover the price'a my tickets for some crap Hollywood love story. 'Cause you write me a check and slip it in my office's mail slot, and I'll leave the padlock to the storeroom's door open. That's unit twenty-four. When you drive in the lot you'll want to pull up to the far end of the building—"

"I know which room it is, Mr. Evers."

"Hey, you don't gotta be short. I'm offerin' to do you a favor here." Evers issued another moist grunt. It suddenly reminded me of a sucking sponge. "You can just latch the door shut when you're through."

I looked at the time again, told him we had a deal, and didn't even bicker over the fact that I was also probably springing for his popcorn and soda. No sense letting Marge's extra pay hang around my pocket long enough to burn a hole in it.

The storage facility was about a quarter mile past the town dump at the South End, and I was there at six on the button. Rollie, however, seemed to have already vacated his office. I didn't see his car parked out front—or any other cars in the lot, for that matter—and there was a CLOSED sign in the door's glass panel. Not that it was any shocker. I'd assumed he'd go lamming out the in-

stant we got off the phone, and had already written his check.

I drove along the low concrete structure to
Abe's unit and backed up to its roll-up door,
thinking that would make it easier to carry the
books and suitcase from the Toyota. Evers had
been good as his parasitic word; the padlock was
open in its hasp. I stopped the SUV, got out, lifted
the cargo hatch, and then went over to raise the
corrugated metal door.

The moment I stepped into the unit I went
stone cold.

Cold throughout my entire body.

Everything inside the room was in disarray—it
looked as if a tornado had blown through it. I saw
books strewn everywhere. Hundreds of books,
many on the floor beside overturned cartons, their
covers flung wide, their dust jackets entirely or
partially off, their pages spread facedown on the
floor. The boxes themselves had lengths of brown
tape straggling from their flaps; I could only guess
Abe must have had them all set to go before someone slashed them open with a knife or a box
cutter.

I gulped down the room's stagnant air and
looked around at the heaps of packing material
scattered over and among the books, tossed from
the shelves on which Abe had kept the stuff. I
saw tape, labels, folded cartons, other supplies. All
over the place.

I didn't know what to think, or do, and just
stood there trying to absorb what I'd stumbled

upon. The room had been ransacked. Somebody had come in and taken it apart. From wall to wall, and corner to corner. *But for what reason?*

It took a while before I got myself under a semblance of control. I wasn't remotely thinking straight, but understood I couldn't stay where I was. And so I moved. At first I didn't have a hint where I was moving to. I just spun dizzily out the doorway and ran like a maniac, past my Toyota and across the parking lot toward Rollie Evers's office. I didn't know why. Not consciously. I suppose I must have had some desperate, irrational hope that he was still around, because the next thing I knew I was pounding on his door and shouting his name as loud as I could. But nobody answered.

I rapped on the door some more, calling for Rollie to come out, my face pressed against the glass pane, my hand rattling the doorknob. Then I finally stopped and tried to get my head on straight. I'd been through worse. Much worse, and barely a week ago. I wasn't going to let myself faint away, not again. This time I had to pull myself together and handle it.

Rollie wasn't in the office. Of course he wasn't. I hadn't really expected to find him around. What I needed to do was get someone else over here. Someone who could help.

Still facing the door, I reached shakily for the cell phone clipped to the waist of my jeans, punched in 911, and waited.

The operator came on after a couple of rings. "Hello, what is your emergency?"

I was about to tell her when I heard an engine revving to life behind me.

"Please tell me the emergency," the operator repeated.

I didn't say anything. Stunned and confused by that sound, I turned my head and stared out toward the end of the building, where I'd left my Toyota with the keys hanging in the ignition . . .

Turned in time to see the SUV tear out of the facility's lot and onto the road, then speed off into the gathering dusk with a loud screech of tires.

"Hello, if someone's on the line, I need you to tell me the emergency!" the 911 operator was insisting urgently.

I opened my mouth, shut it, opened it again.

"Somebody just stole my vehicle," I said, finding my voice at last.

Chapter 11

"So you're sure you didn't get a look at whoever drove off in the SUV?" Chief Vega asked.

I shook my head.

"Or notice anyone hanging around before you heard its motor?"

I shook my head again.

"How about when you first got here? Or went out to the storage unit? Anything in hindsight that might have been a sign you were being watched?"

I gave a third head shake and dabbed my leaky, bloodshot eyes with a Kleenex. Every time he saw me Vega wound up handing out tissues, but probably he was accustomed to that sort of thing. I don't suppose many people who call the police are in a cheery mood.

We stood in the parking area outside Rollie Evers's locked office, Vega holding a pen over his tried-and-true notepad as I struggled not to weep outright. I know I'd promised myself I'd be stronger than that, but when I thought about what I'd lost—what was *inside* the Toyota . . .

As Vega scribbled away on his pad—I wondered what law enforcement shorthand was for "clueless blubberer"—I glanced past him and across the lot at the open storeroom.

Three official cars were pulled up to its raised gate in the fading daylight. The first to arrive had been Vega's black-and-white cruiser. Then, one right behind the other, a couple of unmarked sedans that might not have looked official except for the men who'd gotten out of them. I supposed they were the Boston detectives Marge Millwood told me had been poking around Old Abe's room. Right now, in fact, they were doing the same sort of rigorous snooping inside and outside the storage unit. They didn't seem like a harmonious set, though. The two guys in navy blue suits who'd left the first unmarked car, a shiny new Plymouth, were spit-polished, clean-shaven, and had short, side-parted hair that looked as if it had been cut by the same politically archconservative barber. *We'd like to have that Newt Gingrich–Tom DeLay thing going for us—a scoop over the forehead, extra flat on top, thank you.* Meanwhile, the pair that had stepped from the second car that arrived, a battered old Dodge, weren't nearly as cookie-cutter bland. One had a five o'clock shadow on his cheeks, the other slightly longish hair. And their suits didn't even match, whoa.

I'd seen the two pairs of detectives exchange some words after they drove up, and they hadn't exactly looked thrilled with each other, which made me wonder if they were from separate branches of the BPD—or maybe altogether different agencies. I was also wondering why a three-car, multi-organizational, possibly interdepartmental assortment of plainclothes officers would show up to answer a stolen vehicle report in such an urgent hurry, although it would become obvious once Chief Vega got further along with his line of questioning. Aside from however it might have tied into the murder investigation, I was convinced that nobody was interested in my missing Toyota.

"Sky, I don't recall you telling me that Mr. Monahan rented this storage unit when we last spoke," Vega said, and then flipped back several pages in the pad as if to double-check. "There's nothing in my notes . . ."

"I probably didn't mention it," I said. "That wouldn't have seemed important at the time."

Vega stopped flipping pages and looked at me.

"What about now?" he said. "Do you get a sense it might be?"

"Of course," I said. His question struck me as kind of ridiculous after what had just happened. "I mean, somebody turned the storage room upside down. There has to be a reason."

"Do you have any ideas about it?"

"No," I said. "I don't."

Vega paused. He shifted his attention to the plainclothesmen jostling around the storeroom, stared at them a minute, then faced me again.

"The items you'd driven over from the Millwood Inn . . . the ones you'd cleared out of Mr. Monahan's room . . . you told me they were mostly articles of clothing and toiletries. And the carton of books, of course."

I nodded.

"Those books," he said. "They were old, is that right?"

"Used," I said.

Vega grunted. "Help me with the distinction."

"Old's old," I said with a shrug. "Such as a first printing of a book that came out a long time ago. But a used book could be a recent best seller. Maybe one that somebody's read and doesn't want to hang on to. Or that a library discards because it has other copies and needs to free up shelf space."

"And Mr. Monahan would lug around boxes of these old and used books whenever he traveled?"

I shook my head.

"It isn't as if he was some kind of compulsive, if that's what you're suggesting," I said. "Abe would pick them up while he was driving here on his way from Florida. He'd stop to check out the local papers and circle ads for library sales, garage sales, flea markets—anyplace they might be getting rid of books. And he'd pay bargain prices. I mean a quarter, fifty cents, never more than a couple of dollars apiece." I shrugged. "It gave Abe a kick whenever he stumbled on to hard-to-find books, but he wasn't interested in re-selling them or anything. He bought books because he enjoyed reading them."

Vega's writing hand moved toward his pad again, as if it had gotten bored with doing nothing.

"Let's say he got an unusually good grab," he said, starting a fresh page of notes. "Could he have revealed it to a local collector, maybe gotten it appraised here in Pigeon Cove . . . if for no other reason than to satisfy his curiosity?" He shrugged his shoulders. "You hear wild stories. A housewife cleans out her attic, fills a carton with junk that's been lying around for ages, plops it on the lawn for one of those weekend yard sales. Then somebody else comes along, digs around in the box, and pulls out Ben Franklin's diary or Shakespeare's racy love letters to his girlfriend."

"I think even Abe would've been tempted to part with that stuff," I said, and managed a thin smile. "Every so often he'd come across a book that was truly rare, sure. He'd always tell me about his best catches. On his last visit, I remember him showing off a copy of a novel called *Nightmare Alley*."

"Like the film with Tyrone Power?"

"Right," I said. "That movie was based on a novel, and Abe was ecstatic because he'd hit on a first printing of the hardcover. He said it was from the nineteen forties . . . and that it was one of his best scores."

"Does that mean it would've been pricey on the collectors' market?"

"Guess it depends what you consider pricey," I said. "Abe thought a specialty bookshop might have charged two or three hundred dollars. For him that was a pretty big deal—"

I broke off, suddenly remembering what Jessie had told me about Stu Redman, who ran a bookshop and Internet book-finding service out of his home in town. *Stu detested Abe*, she'd said. Exact words. Still, I wasn't about to let myself get carried away. She'd buzzed about other supposed Abe-haters, too, and I had a feeling she might have overstated things to protect her friend Drecksel. Also, I housecleaned for Stu regularly and he seemed pretty well-heeled, not to mention sane— at least by the Cove's very liberal standards of sanity. It seemed downright idiotic to imagine he would murder Abe, or break into the storage unit, for *Nightmare Alley* or any other book he could have easily afforded to buy. And that was assuming he even knew about Abe stumbling upon the novel or renting the unit.

Id-i-ot-ic.

I tore free of my thoughts and realized Vega was looking at me.

"Was there something you were about to add?" he said.

"No," I said. At that point, it was the truth. It would've been crummy and irresponsible of me to toss Stu's name out at Vega simply because Jessie Barton had mentioned it in the same breath as several others . . . keeping in mind that Jessie was the same woman who'd insisted there was absolutely, positively, certifiably no way her chum and neighbor Bill Drecksel would ever harm a fly.

About a half minute passed quietly. I stood there thinking and watching the plainclothesmen inspect this and that across the lot. I hoped they'd do everything humanly possible to get to the bottom of Old Abe's murder, if that was why they'd showed up. In the meantime, though, it struck me that if any *one* of them—and that included Chief Vega—had bothered to consider why I'd called the police in the first place, they could've probably stopped whoever drove away with my Toyota before he got off the Cape.

"Okay, Sky, let's see if we can wrap this up," Vega said finally. "What I'm wondering . . . that is, can you think of anything here that would have drawn attention from robbers? I mean anything at all of value, whether to Abe Monahan or some other individual?"

At that, my eyes threatened to gush with tears again, and I bunched the tissue against them to dam the flow. It was Vega's choice of words, I suppose.

"My SUV," I said.

"What?" Vega looked as if I'd spoken in a lost Martian dialect.

"My Toyota," I said, thinking that it was not only of value, but had zoomed off into nowhere with something irreplaceably precious to me on its backseat. "It was here, and it was stolen. Or doesn't that concern you?"

At first Vega continued to wear his confused expression. But then he sighed and looked steadily at my face.

"Sky, it's obviously important—"

"Then why aren't you doing something to find it?" I said. "I know you've got a lot on your hands. I want to answer your questions. Even so, I need your help right now. And I hate feeling like I have to remind you."

Vega hesitated, dropped his voice a notch.

"I've got three patrol cars—that's most of my fleet—trying to track down your vehicle. And there's an all-points out across the Cape. But my choice was either to ask the questions myself or leave it up to those self-important hotshots." He tilted his head slightly toward the police detectives, or whatever they were. "Their bedside manner isn't particularly gentle, and I figured I'd run interference." He shook his head, sighed. "Although in hindsight I guess my approach wasn't much better."

I looked at him.

"Chief Vega, do *you* think whoever broke into the storeroom took my SUV? And that it all has some connection to Abe's murder?"

His eyes fixed on mine.

"You're really talking about three linkages, and I'd be lying if I denied any are possible," he said, almost whispering now. "But I think we need to be careful. There are a lot of possibilities to juggle, and we shouldn't just snatch at one of them. Maybe you were a target of opportunity. Somebody could have known Evers was gone and just happened to see you pull up in the Toyota. Maybe whoever stole it didn't even realize the storage room was burglarized. Or maybe he committed both thefts but had no idea whose stuff was inside and never heard of Abel Monahan." He paused. "I hope the Toyota's theft is more innocuous than it seems, if I can use that word about this type of crime. Pigeon Cove is one of the few towns in our state—possibly in the entire country—where joyriders are more often responsible for taking people's vehicles than professional thieves are."

"By joyriders . . . you mean teenagers?"

Vega nodded.

"That certainly would be a best-case scenario," he said. "You get a kid who steals a set of wheels, he'll take his friends for a ride, then ditch it when they're through having their kicks. There's a decent chance the vehicle itself won't be damaged, but I need to be frank—you shouldn't expect to recover any belongings that can be carried off. For example, a cell phone, a CD player, satellite radio, notebook computer, or whatever else they can use, hock, trade, or sell. They'd also very likely toss any items they *don't* have any use for."

I looked at him.

"Toss them *where*?"

"Onto the road, in a Dumpster, wherever. Just to get rid of them fast."

My throat tightened. I could handle losing the Toyota. As much as I loved it and relied on it for getting around, it was replaceable. Nearly everything I owned was. Except for my most cherished possession, which happened to be something I almost always kept in the SUV. That one thing, of all things, could never be replaced. And here Chief Vega was telling me some thieving delinquents would probably want to chuck it out the window like a bag stuffed with greasy junk-food wrappers.

The thought of it pierced my heart.

"What if it *wasn't* kids?" I asked in a cracking voice. "What's that do to my odds of getting the SUV back?"

Vega inhaled, slowly released the breath.

"I'm sorry to say it doesn't improve them," he said. "Do you have theft coverage on your insurance?"

I nodded that I did.

"How about a record of the vehicle identification number?"

I nodded again. "It's at home," I said. "I keep it in a desk drawer."

"Super. That'll help," Vega said. "When a theft's reported, the VIN goes into a national crime database." He paused while taking some more notes. "Another thing to consider . . . and I know it doesn't sound encouraging right off, but there may be a silver lining, so to speak . . . is that a lot of pros in the area do strip-and-runs nowadays. They'll drive over to some isolated spot instead of a chop shop and strip the more easily marketable parts and accessories. Seats, air bags, sections of the engine, you name it. Sometimes they'll disassemble everything but a vehicle's bare outer frame."

"And that's supposed to be a *positive*?"

"A definite one when it comes to expediting your insurance payment," Vega said. "In the case of a strip-and-run, when the insurer contacts the police—namely me—about your claim, I can flat-out confirm that we found the vehicle's abandoned body. It cuts through a lot of red tape. The insurance company won't have to waste time waiting for us to clear the case, or have its own investigators make certain it isn't fraud, or that a claimant's kid or boyfriend didn't take the keys and drive off on a long vacation. All of which are SOP when a vehicle vanishes without a trace."

Chief Vega's face blurred as my eyes flooded with tears. I knew he'd meant to offer me some consolation. I appreciated that. But I'd had a sudden, vivid image of the Toyota picked apart like roadkill after the crows had come and gone . . . and of my bag of tricks, the one reminder of Paul I had always kept close to me, lying squashed in the middle of some two-lane blacktop, with its contents scattered everywhere and tire treads running across it.

"Sky, are you all right?" Vega asked.

I nodded that I was, and then blew it by heaving with sobs, not even bothering to consider Silkian deep-breathing techniques this time around.

A moment later Vega was dispensing more Kleenex from the pack in his breast pocket. I added them to the wad in my hand—which by now was about the size of a cauliflower—and smushed it against my eyes.

"Sorry," I snuffled. I felt overloaded, overwhelmed, over-*everythinged*. "Guess a lot of things've just caught up to me . . ."

The sentence evaporated on my tongue. Although I suppose I'd already gotten out enough of it to make for a good, if not perfect, segue as Mike Ennis's Mini Cooper came swinging into the lot about dozen yards in front of me, where the investigators were still poking around Abe's storage unit.

They swiveled their heads to check out the Cooper. The plainclothesmen, Vega, all of them turned toward it at once.

Since I was already looking straight at it, I didn't have to bother.

Blotting my eyes with the clump of soggy tissues, I watched Mike pull to a halt, slide out the driver's door, and wave his press credential at the detectives. Then one of the guys with the scoop haircut went up to him, shaking his head briskly while they conversed near the parked car. I took the head shake as a reliable sign that Scoop wasn't thrilled by Mike's arrival. Judging by their hostile expressions, none of the detectives were. In fact, they were glowering at Mike like he was a gate crasher at a black-tie affair.

I was thinking maybe I should make a sour face too, just to fit in with the in-crowd. Except, like it or not, seeing Mike made me want to smile. This consequently made me upset with myself, so I frowned anyway. No chance he'd get the merest twitch of a smile out of me. It wasn't as if I thought he'd showed up for my sake. His only reason for being there would be to chase a story, just like he'd been chasing it when he asked me out to dinner under false pretenses.

No, as much as I could have used somebody to lean on at that moment, Mike Ennis was totally the wrong person.

Would you kiss him?

What a stupid question that had been, I thought. So stupid it belonged way up high on the Sky Taylor's All-Time Stupidest Questions list. What I probably should have been asking, in fact, was whether I'd kick him.

I watched Mike stand there with Scoop for a few seconds, figuring he meant to talk his way into the storage unit before the crime scene tape went up, the same as he'd tried talking his way into Abe's room once the tape there went down. But, surprise, he instead started walking quickly across the lot toward Chief Vega and myself.

He gave Vega a nod as he approached.

"Chief," he said.

"Evening, Mike," Vega said. "Guess you've been keeping your PB scanner on."

"I caught the dispatch," Mike acknowledged, and then turned to me. "I'm sorry about the Toyota, Sky. The minute I heard your name on the call, I drove over as fast as I could."

I gave him a stare meant to send icy daggers through him. But I had a hunch my tears had turned the ice kind of slushy.

"If you're after an exclusive interview with the victim, forget it," I said in a clogged voice.

Mike shook his head.

"I came because I was worried about you," he said. "And because I figured you could use a lift back to the Fog Bell."

I didn't believe him. At least, I didn't think I did. If I'd been so much on his mind, why had he gone over to the detectives first?

"Chief Vega's offered to take me home in his patrol car," I said truthfully. "But thanks anyway."

Mike looked at me. I looked at him. Chief Vega raised a dark eyebrow and looked at both of us, as if under the impression that he'd stepped into the middle of something personal. Which, I thought, would be a mistake on his part. As far as I was concerned, when it came to my relationship with Mike, there wasn't anything personal going on for him to step into.

As we continued to exchange glances, Vega sort of backed away a little, almost managing to seem inconspicuous about giving us some space. It was very decent and considerate of him, or so I thought, particularly because he'd been interrupted while conducting police business.

I decided then that I liked police chief Alejandro Vega. He really had been looking out for me.

"Sky, we need to talk," Mike said now, stepping closer. "I have to explain a few things."

My eyes stung worse than they had a second before, but I refused to start blubbering in front of him.

"Swell," I said. "Explain away."

"Not right here," Mike said. "This isn't the place."

I shrugged. "I'll be at the *Anchor* later in the week, assuming my insurance policy covers car rentals."

Mike looked at me some more, cleared his throat.

"Sky, listen, I know you're angry at me about the other night," he said. "I deserve it, and I won't make excuses. But if you could give me a chance—"

I cut him off right there. I'd genuinely had enough.

"You don't get it, do you?" I snapped, tightening my fist around my squishy ball of tissues. "My SUV was stolen from under my nose. That was less than an hour ago, after I found the place where my friend—my *murdered* friend—kept some of his prized possessions completely trashed. Call me selfish, Mike. But at the moment I don't care about giving anyone chances. I'm the one who could use a break."

Silence. Mike held his gaze on me, opened his mouth as if to say something, but seemed to change his mind. He shook his head, looked down at the ground for a long moment. Then, before I could let myself wonder if I'd been too hard on him, he turned to peer across the parking lot at the detectives.

"Those sensitive souls are about ready to start grilling Sky," he told Vega. "Check it out."

Vega glanced their way. So did I. One of the scoop-heads was walking briskly toward us from the storage unit.

"I'll handle it," Vega said, and shifted his attention to me. "You'd better scrunch into my cruiser—the rear door's unlocked. If that guy asks, I'm giving you a lift home because you feel faint, okay?" he said.

I watched the detective come closer, his loafers slapping the blacktop. Though I wasn't sure what reasons Chief Vega and Mike had for disliking him and his friends, I decided on the spot that I wasn't in any rush to find out.

"Okay," I said, and started toward Vega's patrol car.

Chapter 12

As Chief Vega dropped me off at the Fog Bell and then drove on up the street toward the police station, I was wishing for nothing more in the world than to see Chloe. I wasn't even sure that I'd want to talk about the theft of my SUV and cleaning kit—though it would have to come up between us, of course—and I really felt it wouldn't matter if we didn't talk about much of anything at all. The accumulated pressure of the past week had gotten to me, and I only wanted to sit with my best friend, maybe have a cup of hot tea in her parlor, and take it as easy as possible.

Let me ask . . . wouldn't it be nice to always get what you wish for exactly *when* you're wishing for it?

I'd just entered the front yard when I heard a car pull up to the curb behind me. Actually, I was halfway into the yard, one foot on the path and the other still on the sidewalk. I reacted to the sound the way most of us would, pausing to sort of vaguely check it out, and turned my head just in time to see Mike Ennis exit his Mini Cooper.

I stood watching as he came around onto the pavement and then stopped, his back almost against the door of his parked car.

"Sky," he said, "give me a minute. Please."

I let a good part of that minute pass before answering him.

"Don't tell me you plan on renting a room here," I said then.

He gave an infinitesimally small smile.

"You know of any rooms being available?" he said.

I shook my head.

"There are no present vacancies," I said.

We stood there facing each other. It was almost sundown, and behind Mike the sky had shaded a deep grayish blue over the high, steeply angled rooftops of the graceful old homes across the street.

"Go on, Mike," I said. "Say what you have to say."

"I starts with 'I'm sorry,' " he said. "But a lot of what I need to tell you comes afterward."

I didn't say anything. In the street, a couple of kids rode past on bicycles. They were eleven, twelve, tops, and I noticed one of them talking into one of those cell phone headsets as they whooshed by. Could be he was negotiating a potential raise in his allowance.

"Chloe has a picnic table in the backyard," I said. "If you like, we can talk there."

Mike stared down at his shoes the way he had in the lot outside Rollie's office. Then he raised his chin, little by little, and looked at me.

"There are some things you need to know about Abe Monahan," he said. "We'll have more privacy in the car."

I blinked. Abe? What could he have to say about *Abe*? I didn't know why Mike's tone made me apprehensive, but it did, and for a while I didn't respond, or budge from where I stood with my heel still on the gravel path leading up through the Fog Bell's blossoming garden.

At last I found myself nodding. I stepped off the path and crossed the sidewalk to the Cooper. Mike opened its passenger door for me, went around to enter through the driver's side, turned on the ignition, and pressed a button to shut the windows. It got warm inside quickly and he put on the air.

"My worst mistake the other night was not getting right to it, and I won't make that mistake again," he said once he'd settled in. "I'll start talking. If you want me to stop for any reason, or need ask any questions, let me know."

I sat beside Mike feeling that unexplainable anxiety, and thinking the Cooper was too small to be anxious in. An SUV was built for anxious. Or a van. The general idea being that you ought to be afforded plenty of room to squirm around in your seat.

I took a breath. Actually, I took a couple of breaths—long, deep ones. Breathing, you see, didn't require much interior space. Then, a bit less tense, I sat some more. There was an outdated inspection sticker on Mike's windshield that needed to be stripped off, leave it to me to notice it. But maybe noticing it was a stall, a way to avoid letting Mike know I was ready for him to go on . . . which I finally did with a slow nod.

"Abe Monahan never existed," he said. "At least, he wasn't the person everybody in Pigeon Cove thought they knew."

"Stop!" I said.

"Sky—"

I made a slicing gesture. "I said, 'Stop,' and you told me if I did that you'd stop."

Mike sat quietly, resting his hand on the steering wheel.

I looked back at him and swallowed.

"Okay," I croaked. My throat was dry as sandpaper. "I was just testing. Start."

Mike met my gaze steadily. "Abe's name—his real name—was Tony Skibaldi."

"Stop!" I said. "No, wait. Question. Skibaldi . . . you mean, as in Skiball with an added syllable?"

Mike gave a slow nod.

"One that ends in a vowel," he said. "Antonio Skibaldi was originally from Sicily, a village on the edge of Palermo where the Cosa Nostra controlled everything. After World War Two he came to this country as an orphan—I think he was in his teens—and moved in with some cousins on Chicago's South Side. That's when he fell into the only way of life he knew. Starting with street gangs, then graduating." Mike paused, his eyes still on mine. "Tony was a mobster, Sky. I wish there was some way to tiptoe around that word, but there isn't. He belonged to the LoCicero family for over thirty years and eventually became one of its top soldiers. Built up quite a rap sheet floating between different crews. Counterfeiting and document forgery, loan-sharking, illegal gambling, running black-market cigarettes. At one point in the late sixties, he served five years in Leavenworth for a racketeering conviction. That's where he hooked up with a Mafia boss named Thomas Navarro . . . better known as Knuckles Navarro."

"Stop!" I shook my head in disbelief. Old Abe a *jailbird*? It was almost unthinkable. And that hoodlum Mike claimed he'd met in prison—I suddenly realized the name sounded familiar.

"Knuckles Navarro . . . isn't he the one who married that famous British pop singer?"

"Zena Lisbon, right," Mike said. "This was after Navarro got out of the slammer in 'seventy-two or thereabouts. She was half his age, something like twenty-five years old, and rumored to be on the wild side. Which was proved out soon enough, when she got caught having an extramarital affair with one of Illinois's respected elder statesmen, Senator Nash Bridgeton."

My heart was beating. That rang a bell, too. "There were those photos of them naked together at some kind of swingers' bash in Aspen, right?"

"Actually, it was Rio de Janeiro," Mike said. "Be that as it may, it was the kind of ongoing public-scandal-slash-soap-opera that the tabloids feed on for months. It was also what indirectly pushed Navarro to mastermind a Brinks truck heist, the largest in history to that point. Besides Knuckles, who wasn't physically seen anywhere near the truck, there were three men involved in the hijack. Its take was reported to have been somewhere between eight and ten million dollars."

"Stop."

Mike looked at me.

"I don't know why I said that," I told him. Although I really did. I was afraid of what was coming next. Terribly afraid. "Go," I said after a second.

Mike nodded again.

"According to prosecutors, Knuckles had planned the robbery for the love of Zena Lisbon, who'd asked for a divorce after her affair hit the news. All the negative publicity had made her want to head back across the pond," he said. "Navarro refused. Sordid fling or no sordid fling, he was obsessed with Zena and figured pulling off the job would impress her—not to mention swell his bankroll—enough to persuade her to stick around." Mike shrugged. "Now let's cut ahead a year or so. The police arrest one of the hijackers for the crime, a sort of knockaround guy with a gambling jones and a big mouth named Al Munion. About ten seconds after he's nabbed, Munion informs on the others. Mostly he does it in exchange for a plea bargain, but he's also got a beef with one of his fellow thieves—the wheelman—

who he claims has bolted with over twice his share of the loot." Mike gave another shrug. "In the end, Knuckles did okay. Though he was supposedly shorted on the loot, and Zena *did* eventually return to London, his trial ends with a complete acquittal. Either there's insufficient evidence to nail him for being the brains behind the whole thing, or he knows how to get to jurors, take your pick. I suppose the arguable weakness in the feds' case is that nobody ever puts Navarro at the scene of the crime." Mike shifted in his seat to look straight at me. "John Brazzo, one of the three wiseguys identified as having seized the truck, isn't as fortunate. He's convicted in a separate trial and does a long stretch behind bars. Which leaves the wheelman, who's gotten away clean with his money."

Mike was quiet. I waited for him to continue, but he just sat there scrutinizing my features.

I turned my head away and looked out the windshield. I tried to ignore the inspection sticker on its upper-left-hand corner, but my eye kept picking at it anyway. I found the sticker to be very aggravating. Really, I wondered, how easy would it be remove it? Soak a cotton square with Goo Gone, dab it onto the sticker, and let it sit for a few minutes. Nothing more to it than that—the sticker would peel off without any gluey residue. I'd have done it myself if I could have gotten out the bottle of Goo Gone I carried with the rest of the supplies in my bag of tricks. But I couldn't.

I didn't have it.

I didn't have my bag of tricks.

I sighed, leaned my head against the backrest, and continued staring out the windshield. Dusk had settled over Pigeon Cove, its shadows flowing together in wide pools along Main Street. I wondered if the kids on bikes were home yet. I hoped they were; boys their age didn't belong out riding as the dark of night set in. I also hoped the one with the cell phone would put the stupid thing aside and forget about it for at least another decade. They deserved their childhood while it lasted, because when it was gone, it was gone.

"You're telling me that Abe, or Tony Skibaldi, is the fourth man, the one who was never caught," I said after a prolonged silence. "That he's a thief who double-crossed his partners—took the stolen money, and ran."

"Yes," Mike said. "I can also tell you Navarro's very much alive, kicking, and in control of a powerful midwestern crime syndicate. And that he still might be trying to recover the missing loot, or whatever's left of it after three-plus decades. Judging by Skibaldi's simple lifestyle, I've got a strong suspicion there's quite a bit."

"Stop, Mike," I said. "Please stop. Abe always seemed like such a good man."

"People change in thirty years."

"But thirty years doesn't change what he did, if the things you're claiming about him are true," I said. "I need to understand . . . I need to *know* . . .

how you can be so certain that he and Tony Skibaldi were one and the same person."

Mike sat quietly again. I still felt his eyes on me.

"My police contacts told me the forensics
revealed it almost by accident," he said. "Abe's
fingerprints were taken so they could be differen-
tiated from others in his room. There's a national
electronic system called AIFIS that would have
routinely compared them to millions of criminal
prints on file in two hours. As they were pro-
cessed, they were found to be a ten-print match
with Skibaldi's."

I almost said "Stop" again, but it was too late.
I think we both realized we were suddenly past
that.

"And what about those other prints? Did any
of them belong to Knuckles Navarro?"

"No. But it's never been his style to do his own
dirty work. If he'd tracked Skibaldi down, it
would have been through a mob soldier or a
hired hand."

I shook my head.

"I don't get it," I said. "If Navarro wanted the
money, what sense would it make for him to have
Abe killed? I mean, if Abe was the only person
who knew where it was stashed?"

"That's a good question," Mike said. "Maybe
Navarro held a grudge and ordered his stooge to
find the cash and take care of Skibaldi at the same
time. I don't know. But I'm guessing he never got
his hands on the money."

I gave that some thought and then finally turned to Mike.

"Because Abe's storage unit was ransacked as if he was looking for it there," I said. "Is that why?"

Mike nodded.

"Yes," he said. "And for another reason besides. Whatever happened at the Millwood, the killer left Skibaldi's room in a hurry. Say he'd been sniffing around it for clues to where the Brinks loot might be stashed. It might've occurred to him that the next person to enter the room got his—or her—hands on it instead."

My heart skipped a beat.

"You're talking about me," I said.

"It would explain why your SUV was stolen. He could have been searching through the storage unit and come up empty. Then, when you arrived, he might have hung around to see if anything in the carton and suitcase you'd brought would lead him to the money, or even whether the money itself was inside them. Those detectives and feebs flocking around the storeroom told me you'd left the Toyota's keys in its ignition, so he would've had a perfect opportunity to jump in and drive away."

"Feebs?"

"FBI agents," Mike said. "The original Brinks hijack crossed state lines and involved bank currency. That automatically makes this a reopening of an old federal investigation."

I digested that, and everything else. From beginning to end, there was nothing good in what I'd learned. And the thought of a murderer skulking around the storage unit, watching my every move from somewhere out of sight, made my skin crawl. But I had another question that had to be answered.

"Mike, did you know about Abe when we were at Linaria?"

He nodded in the affirmative.

"I wanted to share the information. But my police contacts had given it to me in strict confidence."

"Chief Vega, you mean?"

"I can't say, Sky."

"But he's in the loop now."

"Let's put it this way . . . I don't think that would be an unreasonable assumption on your part." Mike paused, then went on slowly. "It matters to me that you know why I pushed to get into Abe's room. I'm a reporter, yes. And there's undeniably a story here. I've had to be aggressive covering stories before, and it's become a reflex I need to watch out for, because it can be hurtful to people who don't deserve it. It was to you. I regret that, and I want to apologize. But for me the story has been secondary—by far—to finding a murderer who's on the loose and could put you in potential jeopardy. You don't have to believe it. I've given you no reason to trust me. It's the truth, though. On my word."

We were quiet for a while. I let my eyes linger on Mike's face, then turned and stared out the windshield.

"My late husband gave me a present on our

first wedding anniversary," I said. "Paul saw a tool case in a hardware store and knew it would make a perfect carrier for my cleaning supplies. I was always a little extreme about cleanliness and order. You could say it's a quirk, I guess. When things around me are right, and in place, it gives me a kind of inner stillness. I don't know how else to put it."

My voice caught, and I swallowed and kept looking straight ahead.

"Your husband was sharper than most men—or maybe I should only speak for myself," Mike said. "I freely admit I'd have bought a necklace, perfume, flowers . . . the gifts you sort of *expect* a woman would want."

"They can be wonderful, don't get me wrong," I said. "But when Paul brought me the tool case, it was the first time I'd felt anybody valued a part of me that usually drives people up the wall."

Again we were silent as the last of the daylight trickled away outside the car.

"That tool bag—my cleaning kit—was in my SUV," I said, my eyes moistening. "There are other vehicles. But some things are special and dear to me. And when they're lost, it hurts like hell."

I stopped talking. I was tired of being sad, tired of crying. I didn't want to break down and have to smother my face with tissues again.

I breathed hard, trying to collect myself, and as I struggled, felt Mike's hand touch my arm.

He gave it a gentle squeeze and let go.

After a moment I turned from the night outside the windshield and looked at him.

"Thank you," I said, and closed my eyes and tilted my forehead down onto his shoulder.

I let it rest there for a very long time.

Chapter 13

"It strikes me that a brand-new Mustang convertible would be fabulous," Chloe Edwards was saying. "Torch red. With woven vanilla bucket seats, or soft, creamy beige leather, providing that's an option."

I looked at her. It was the morning after my SUV had been stolen, and we were having coffee at her backyard picnic table in the dappled shade of a tall old oak tree. We'd started our conversation in her dining room, but Oscar was in one of his tooting frenzies, and we'd decided to move it and our breakfast muffins outside where we could hear ourselves talk.

"Maybe we should set our sights on something that's, ah, a smidge less flashy," I said.

Chloe raised her steaming cup, sipped, and then lowered it to the slatted wooden table.

"I wouldn't think to impose my tastes on you, dear. I realize they can be frivolous at times," she said. "Let's pass on the soft top. A sunroof would be fine. Or a moonroof. To be candid, I've never managed to figure out the difference between them." She tapped her chin with a forefinger. "If we're going for subdued, how about an Atlantic-Ocean-blue car? It's richer and deeper than the Pacific blue. Or do you prefer a pearl white exterior? Or lime green, like my Beetle? In any case, we should stick with light-colored seats, since they'll stay cooler when you park it in the hot sun."

I drank some coffee, broke off a piece of an apple-cinnamon muffin, and ate. Oscar struck a high, sustained note on his clarinet, startling some little brown finches from a nearby bayberry shrub.

Hope there are no hornet nests around for him to stir up, I thought as the birds dispersed in a flutter. The last time Oscar had riled the hornets, it had cost Chloe some regular guests at the inn and almost brought on a damage suit when one of them got stung.

"Any other makes or models grab you?" I urged her. "Just in case we need to find a more practical alternative."

Chloe took another drink from her cup.

"If you're leaning toward fuel efficiency, it might be exciting to try out a Prius," she said. "I've developed an interest in hybrid technology, did I tell you?"

"Ixnay on the Prius," I said before we could fall off the beam. "Any other suggestions? Think basic, Chloe."

She tapped her chin thoughtfully.

"A Lexus sports-utility vehicle is as basic a

rental as *I'd* consider in your shoes." she said. "It's practical yet classy."

I looked at Chloe and chewed a bite of my muffin. I didn't know if she'd ever had any experience renting an automobile. My educated guess was that she hadn't. At least not outside of Chloe World, where flying cars like they'd had on those old Jetsons cartoons were probably commonplace. Still, I was hoping to gently impart the message that Nick and Frankie Mack's Auto Rentals on Route 128—which happened to be the nearest approved service on my policy's list—wouldn't have any Mustang, Prius, or Lexus vehicles available. Not to mention Maseratis, Jaguars, or DeLoreans.

"I feel we'd better lean more toward the mundane when it comes to our choices," I said. "An Escort, say. Maybe an Outback. Or a regular station wagon—now that would be practical."

Chloe pulled a face.

"But not the slightest bit classy. A rental company should have *something* stylish to offer," she said. "It's too bad you're stuck with those Mack brothers, who skimp on investing in their business even more than their parents used to."

I sighed.

"Tell you what, Chloe. We'll wait till we see what's in their lot this afternoon, okay?"

Chloe regarded me over the rim of her cup.

"That sounds fine," she said. "All I suggest is that you stay open to different possibilities, Sky. You know, when Oscar and I were young, we owned a 'fifty-seven Corvette roadster. Only six thousand of them were made, imagine that! It had an Arctic blue body, coral side coves, chrome trim galore. And let me tell you, driving around in it was a blast." She smiled a little at the recollection. "A snazzy hot rod—even a rental—can do wonders for one's morale. Get up, get out into something new, as the song goes."

Now I found myself smiling too.

"I'll keep your advice in mind," I said.

"Promise?"

"Promise."

Some time passed. The day had gotten off to a gorgeous start, with the combination of a fresh crisp breeze, oodles of sunshine, and Chloe's magical personality helping to clear away some of my inner gloom.

We sat drinking our coffees and eating Chloe's scrumptious homemade muffins from the tray she'd set out in front of us. Inside his study, Oscar attacked his mouthpiece to produce a shivering vibrato that made my ears twitch. Although my apartment was upstairs at the opposite end of the house, I heard Skiball let out a big, loud bellow. I hadn't lived with her long enough to be sure whether she was singing along or scared stiff, though I had a weird feeling it might be the former. So far I'd noticed that she liked to bounce on a chair to rap, pop her claws into the mattress to rock, and roll on the rug to cool jazz, leading me to conclude that her musical tastes were kind of eclectic.

"You're sure it's okay that I borrow your VW

today?" I asked Chloe after a while. "I'd hate for you to blow your whole morning on my account."

Chloe flapped a hand at me.

"Don't worry at all," she said. "I have to stick around here and prepare a room for some guests."

She reached into her sweater pocket for a spare set of keys and handed them to me.

"So," she said, "tell me what errands you intend to run."

"My first port of call is Stu Redman's," I said. "I have an appointment to clean his place the day after tomorrow, and wanted to let him know in person that I'll have to postpone all my bookings until, well . . ."

I can buy myself a new cleaning kit, I thought.

"You restock your professional supplies," Chloe offered, sparing me from having to mouth the painful words.

I wanted to hug her. I also wanted to tell her the truth about why I was paying Stu a visit. But before getting out of his car last night, I'd promised Mike I would keep that a secret.

Our plan called for me to visit the bookshop, while he was to talk with Stu's fellow Abe-hater, Noel Lawless.

"I only have one favor to ask, if it isn't too inconvenient," Chloe said. "On your way back here, could you stop at the August Moon? Jessie's been working on the latest version of the La-dee-das' repertoire on her computer. She promised to have it printed out today and said she'd bring it to work with her."

"Not a problem." I checked my wristwatch, realized it was almost twenty past nine, and stood up, brushing a few stray crumbs off my blouse. "Better get my act in gear," I said.

I gave Chloe a hand gathering our cups and dishes onto the breakfast tray and carried it inside the house. Then I went up to my room, fetched my purse, rubbed the tip of my nose against Skiball's to wish her a pleasant day and, once I heard her start to purr, went whizzing off.

The Edwardses' garage faced Carriage Lane, which ran across the north wing of the house to intersect with Main Street. I went down to it using a side door, got into the Beetle, and carefully backed out the short driveway.

It was as I was turning onto the road that I saw a small white car charge—and I mean really *charge*—from the curb up ahead of me near the corner of Main. I watched it whip around to the right at the intersection and frowned. Vehicles were zooming away from me wherever I went these days, or so it seemed.

I suppose it gave me a flashback to the night before, because I felt sort of creeped out afterward. Though it wasn't exactly like I was a post-traumatic stress case . . . in fairness to myself, you didn't see many people speeding in the Cove. Also, Carriage Lane was the narrowest street in town, and to prevent traffic jams the police had imposed an alternate-side-parking—and concurrent no-standing—restriction that started at eight a.m. and ensured that one curb was always clear. This was the day for Chloe's side of the street to be free of cars, meaning that the one I saw couldn't have been there very long. Chief Vega was strict about enforcing the ordinances, even with day-trippers. Sit at the curb more than fifteen minutes, you'd get shooed away.

Ah, well, I thought. At least this time the driver was in his own vehicle rather than mine.

I cruised toward the intersection and made a right turn into the cloud of exhaust left by the white car's tailpipe. Well, okay, I josh with you. It didn't quite leave behind a trail of smoke. But it'd sounded like it should have, and I drove more slowly than usual to compensate for the uncivilized speeder behind its wheel. That's the sort of upstanding townsperson I am.

Stu Redman's bookshop, Redbooks, was on the first floor of his nineteenth-century American Foursquare on Willow Drive, a cul-de-sac several hilly turns and a looping curve or three back of Main Street. Its tucked-away location accounted for the lack of walk-in trade that had prompted Stu to expand into online selling, though everyone in town figured he mostly got by on a private income—i.e., a family inheritance. Still, he was serious about his business, and particular about keeping the shop as well ordered as any public library—something that I figured would aid my mission as I did some nosing around.

I swung up a steep drive into the parking area in front of the house, where Stu had painted slots for three or four vehicles on the blacktop—what did I tell you about his being organized? Except for the slot reserved for his van, they were all unoccupied. I took my pick, got out of the Beetle, and went over to the porch entrance, remembering my last conversation with Mike.

In spite of everything I'd learned about Abe—I couldn't think of him as Tony Skibaldi, and doubted I ever would—there still wasn't a shred of evidence that his former partner in crime, Knuckles Navarro, was responsible for his murder. And when I'd decided to tell Mike about Jessie's finger-pointing at Stu and Noel Lawless, making him promise to hold off on relaying her comments to the police till we were reasonably convinced they had some merit, he'd maintained that we had an obligation to look at every angle ourselves in the meantime.

Since I had a perfect excuse to drop by Stu Redman's place, we'd figured he would be my responsibility. Meanwhile, Mike had gone to see Noel, whom he had gotten to know a little when she'd written some editorials for the *Anchor*.

Now I pushed open the front door, heard the clutch of bells overhead jingling. I was silently running book titles and their authors through my mind, all of which were attached to Abe's most favorite and bragged-about finds—those I'd been able to remember, anyhow. There were considerably more than a few.

About the size of an ocean liner, Stu's desk loomed just inside the door. As I entered, he was in his chair behind it, busily tagging books from the precarious stacks hemming it in on all sides.

"Sky Taylor . . . why, top a' the day, lass," Stu said in an Irish brogue that was rumored to be affected, since it was common knowledge he'd been born and raised in Flatbush, Brooklyn, and was of Ashkenazic Jewish descent. "I'm surprised to see you—we don't have an appointment, or am I mistaken?"

He started reaching for his desk calendar.

"No need to check, Stu," I said with a pleasant smile. "I'm not due for a couple of days."

Stu's eyebrows arched as he drew himself upright. He was a tall, broad-chested man wearing a tan sport coat, a checkered blue-and-white shirt, and an ascot, with a craggy, red-blotched face framed by a gray Melvillian beard and a bulbous nose covered with a fine lattice of broken blood vessels. Stu, word had it, held his double dark Dublin stout in the highest esteem—and unlike his accent, the malt was the real alcohol-saturated deal.

"Ah," he said, "I'm puzzled, then. What can I do for you?"

"Actually, I was right in the area and figured I'd come by to tell you I'll need to rearrange my schedule," I said.

"Ah," Stu said again. He pulled at his varicose nose. "I heard you were the first to discover that unfortunate event at the Millwood Inn."

"If you mean Abel Monahan's murder," I said, "yes, I was."

"And how are you doing, poor girl?"

"As well as can be expected," I said. "Some things have happened to me since, and I need to take care of them."

"Ah." Stu gave me a look. "I don't mean to pry, but am I to assume the reason for your re-arrangement is associated with the event?"

"Yes, it is," I said. I didn't elaborate. I wasn't inclined to mention my Toyota having been stolen—it was too draining to repeat the story. And the way news traveled in the Cove, he'd hear about it fast enough.

Stu pulled on his nose some more, his forehead wrinkling. I took the opportunity to eye the piles of books he'd been tagging.

"A shame about Monahan," he said after a moment. "He was a rare-book enthusiast, as you may have heard."

"No, I didn't," I lied outright. "That is, it isn't something we ever talked about."

"Oh? I'd heard the two of you were close."

I shrugged. I wasn't sure how much Stu knew about my relationship with Abe. The less I revealed about it, though, the better chance I had of getting a sense of *their* relationship. And that was part of why I'd driven to his store in the first place—the other part being to take a peek at the contents of his shelves.

"We were friendly, sure," I said. "He was a nice man, and I'd chat with him now and then whenever he visited town. But he didn't discuss many of his personal interests with me."

"Well, Abel Monahan had a talent for finding rarities," Stu said. "He could pull the single nugget of gold from a bog of mud, aye."

Aye. From a Flatbush boy.

"Come to think, I did notice him reading a lot," I said. "He used to like sitting in the parlor at the Millwood Inn with a book on his lap."

"At the inn and elsewhere around town," Stu said. "I hesitate to speak ill of the dead, but his carelessness often vexed me."

I looked at him.

"How's that?"

Stu gestured toward a doorless entryway to his right. On the far side of it was a large browsing room, all four walls of which were lined with old-fashioned legal bookcases that were crammed with stock.

"I believe rare books belong behind glass, not exposed to human and environmental grubbiness," he said. "Any knowledgeable bibliophile would share that sentiment, I'd venture."

"And Abe didn't?"

Stu shook his head. "You'll notice I called him an enthusiast, not a true-to-the-bone collector," he said. "There's a distinction—and I made it to his face. A collector would never bring a first impression of Hillerman's *Listening Woman* to Gull Wing wharf for an afternoon of reading, yet that's what Abel Monahan did. Gull Wing wharf! Where seabirds wheeling high over the waterfront benches are apt to spatter their oily droppings upon the pages of an open book."

I found his description weirdly picturesque, but that was beside the point.

"Did you ever discuss that with him?" I asked.

"Discuss? We had a bloody public row on the Wing. Shouting and all. 'Why do you need a first printing just to *read* a book?' I asked. I offered to pay top dollar for it, even replace it with a later edition. But the stubborn cuss rejected me, ach!"

It seemed to me that Stu's questionable brogue had thickened as he grew more excited.

"Doesn't sound as if you cared for Abe much," I said.

Stu straightened behind the desk again.

"I beg your pardon, lass!" he said. "Abel Monahan and I may have knocked heads here and there, but he loved the written word with a passion, and I respected that about him."

Which made me wonder if Jessie had completely misread—no pun intended—Stu Redman's feelings about Abe. Or defensively exaggerated them to cover for her friend Drecksel, as I'd surmised before. Either that or Stu was trying to do the opposite and downplay his level of resentment. Instinct told me he was being upfront, though.

At any rate, I knew I had to stop with the questions before Stu got so worked up he became unintelligible. It was time to shift into Phase Two of my act and make a hurried round of the browsing room.

"If it's okay, I want to look over your bookcases before I leave," I said. "I'm replenishing my cleaning supplies today, and want to see what I'll need next time I tidy them up."

Stu swept his hand toward the browsing room.

"There's a thoroughly professional woman for you!" he said. "Be my guest—we must keep everything shipshape."

I turned into the room and went straight over to the legal cases, back to mentally reviewing the titles and authors of Abe's top grabs. His most prized books had been novels, and Stu's fiction section was along the wall to my right, with the books on the shelves arranged alphabetically by author.

I started with "G" for William Lindsay Gresham, who'd written *Nightmare Alley*.

"Seems I'll need some glass cleaner for panels," I called out to Stu, scanning a row of book spines. The only thing by Gresham was a book called *Limbo Tower*, nothing Abe had ever mentioned to me.

I moved on. There were several Hillermans, but no *Listening Woman*. What else? *Dead City* by Shane Stevens. And another novel he'd written . . . I couldn't recall the title but was positive it'd be familiar if I spotted it.

"I'd better pick up some metal polish too—I see smudges on a few of these knobs," I announced, finding a copy of a book called *By Reason of Insanity* in the Stevens section. That was it—the novel Abe had raved about, but I could tell right off it was a different copy. The dust jacket on Redman's book was sort of ragged, with a tear on the bottom of the spine. Abe's had looked almost brand-new.

"Floor polish, furniture polish, soft rags," I said loud enough for a deaf person to hear, aware that I was overcompensating ridiculously for sneaking around.

I tried to remember more titles. So far I hadn't found a single book that Stu might have lifted from Abe's storeroom. What else was there?

Blackboard Jungle, I thought. By Evan Hunter.

I rushed over to the "H" shelf. Abe had always praised Evan Hunter to the moon and stars. Said he'd been the last of a breed, and one of the best American novelists of our time, maybe one of the most influential *ever* . . .

There was no *Blackboard Jungle* in the Hunter section, which took up almost an entire shelf. But hadn't he written under another pen name as well?

I paused a second, thinking furiously. McCain? No. McCann? Uh-uh. What was it? Wait. McBain. Bingo.

Ed McBain. The best, in Old Abe's eyes.

I'd just knelt to find the beginning of the "M" section when I heard the tinkling of the door chimes.

"Halloo," Stu said to whoever had entered the shop. "This makes twice that you've visited me since you've been in town—isn't that so, boyo?"

"Yes," the caller said. "I was out for a walk, and thought I'd see if you were open."

The voice sound familiar, though I couldn't place it. Still squatting down to look at the bookcase's bottom shelf, I glanced curiously into the next room.

My eyes widened. In fact, it felt as if they'd suddenly bulged out of my head.

Adam Kennedy stood at the desk, his head turned toward the browsing room.

Turned to look at me.

"Sky Taylor," he said, and lowered his gaze to my face. "Good morning."

I stood up, went to the entry between the two rooms.

"You two have met?" Stu said from his desk.

Kennedy nodded.

"At the Millwood Inn, where I'm staying," he said with a smile. "And enjoying the early breakfast buffets."

"Well, lives are chains of chances, they say!"

His sports sunglasses hooked over the collar of his golf shirt, Kennedy fastened his glacial eyes on me as he extended his hand.

"It does seem that we keep crossing paths," he said. "But it could be that isn't as great a coincidence as it seems."

"Oh?" I said, short of any other remotely articulate response.

Kennedy nodded.

"When I'm in a town that's new to me, I like to get out and feel its pulse. And with you obviously being an active person, we're bound to find ourselves in the same spot time and again."

I pulled my hand away from his. It was almost a replay of our introduction at Marge's—except that now my reaction to his touch was almost indescribably more intense. A hard frost seemed to have formed in my stomach.

I looked over at Stu Redman, wanting to hurry my exit.

"Well, I'm on to run some errands," I said. "We'll talk in a couple of days, when I'm ready to reschedule my appointments."

"Fine, lassie," he said. "You know where to reach me."

I gave Kennedy a polite see-you-around and left the shop.

Pulling the car out of Stu's drive, I paused to look both ways before turning onto Willow. The nearest cross street was to my right. To the left was a row of homes leading toward a dented metal rail marking the cul-de-sac's dead end. I noticed that somebody had parked a small white car there, parallel to the rail. A Nissan, I saw, taking a closer look.

I told myself it wasn't the same car I'd seen pull away outside the Fog Bell.

I told myself it wasn't Kennedy's car.

I was out for a walk, he'd said to Stu.

I told myself it wasn't his car again and made the right off Willow, and by the time I got back to Main Street had almost convinced myself I was being far, far too paranoid. About the car, and about the notion that there was anything strange or sinister about Kennedy.

Before heading over toward Jessie's for the La-dee-das' song list, I turned in the opposite direction, drove to the service station near the commuter rail-road stop, and gave the Beetle a fill-up, a deluxe drive-through wash, and an interior vacuuming. Knowing there wasn't the slightest chance Chloe would accept gas money from me, it was the only way without an argument that I could pay her back for lending me the car.

The Beetle clean, wax-shined, and topped off to the brim, I went back along Main toward the Gull Wing. Over half an hour had passed since I'd left Stu Redman's. I could see seabirds up ahead over the docks, gliding in the morning breeze as they got ready to drop their poop bombs on unwary readers. The thought not only made me smile but helped shake off any residual weird feelings that might have lingered as the result of my bumping into Adam Kennedy.

When I reached the Autumn Moon, I saw the CLOSED sign in the door. That surprised me a bit, though I guessed it shouldn't have. It was almost eleven a.m., later than Jessie usually opened, but her hours could be quirky.

I pulled over in front of the store and looked through the window. The lights were off, and I saw no sign of Jessie inside. I sat a minute, wondering if I ought to hang out for a while or take care of some other odds and ends in town and try catching her afterward. On the other hand, I thought, it might make sense to drive around to the public parking lot running behind all the shops on the Wing. Most storekeepers had rear entrances there so they could lure customers in from both sides, but Jessie used her back door strictly for loading and unloading merchandise. Maybe she'd be outside her stockroom primping for some handsome truck driver who'd rolled up from Boston or New York to make a delivery.

It seemed worth a shot.

I angled away from the curb, looped around behind the stores, and turned into the lot. There were only a few scattered vehicles around, and I cut across an empty row of slots toward the back of Jessie's shop. No luck. Her rear entrance was shut, and her car wasn't in sight. Nor were any truck drivers outside, hunky or otherwise.

That almost sealed it as far as convincing me to try again later. But then I figured I'd might as well knock on the back door.

I pulled into a spot directly behind the store, got out of the Beetle, strolled up to the door, and rapped on it. Nobody answered. I waited a minute, knocked again. Nothing, nobody. I turned and started walking back toward the Beetle.

An instant later I stopped and sucked in a breath, staring across the lot.

A small white car was parked farther on toward the waterfront.

And so what? I told myself. *What of it?* I was supposed to be over my paranoia. It was a fine day, the salt breeze off the harbor delightful, the poop birds flying high and happy over the wharf. Forget the white car. There were a lot of white cars in town. White was a very popular choice among conscientious, law-abiding automobile buyers the world over. There was no reason to think the white car across the lot was at all suspicious.

Except I didn't really believe that. I tried, but I didn't. Because it was hard to deny it looked a whole lot like the white car I'd already seen twice that morning.

I decided to walk a little closer to the car so I could see what kind it was. The one on Willow Drive had been a Nissan. If this one proved to be a Plymouth or a Dodge, it would be a simple deduction that it was, indeed, a different car, ending my internal debate before I started pulling my hair out.

I'd taken a step or two forward when the smell of lousy coffee came wafting toward me from my right. I was thinking I'd recognize that offensive odor anywhere. Drecksel's Special Blend wasn't only a tongue curdler, it was a torment to the nose. Which made it immediately identifiable, if nothing else.

I was, I realized, standing behind Drecksel's Diner. The back door was wide open as Bill brewed a pot, meaning he either wanted to attract customers to the diner from the parking lot or, more likely, give any flies trapped inside a humane means of evacuation.

I glanced over my shoulder through the door, saw Drecksel behind the front register. He was talking to some guy with a take-out bag while he rang him up.

As I paused momentarily to look in, the customer took a quick, sidelong glance out into the lot. Even as he went on talking, his gaze landed on me, held for a moment, then returned to Drecksel.

I went cold. It wasn't just my stomach this time. It was everywhere, an all-over cold I was irrationally afraid would freeze me solid where I stood.

The customer was Adam Kennedy. I had recognized him at once. And I had no doubt in my mind that the recognition had been mutual.

I told myself to get moving before I turned to ice. Not toward the white car now; I didn't need to see it close up anymore. My curiosity had been satisfied in the most frightening way possible.

I wanted to run to the Beetle as fast as I could, but something told me not to let Kennedy know how unnerved I was. So I walked to the car without making myself too conspicuous, got in, pulled out of the lot, and then turned back onto the road and drove off the Wing.

I kept going, passing street after street, driving halfway through town before I finally pulled over, reached for my cell phone, and tapped in Mike's number.

He answered on the second ring.

"Sky, what's happening?"

I let him know. About the white car and Adam Kennedy, and the morning I'd first run into him and his uncle on the quarry trail, and our second meeting at the Millwood. I spilled it all out to Mike in a blubbering rush, right on through my encounter with Kennedy at Stu's and then seeing him at Drecksel's Diner.

"I'm scared of that man. I really am," I concluded. "It's like he shows up everywhere I go."

"And you're saying he's the same guy who's booked Monahan's old suite at the inn? The one Marge Millwood told you specifically requested it?"

"Yes," I said in a trembling voice. "Mike, what do you think we should do?"

There was a long, long pause at the end of the line.

And then he told me.

Chapter 14

"I think maybe we should be having second thoughts," I whispered.

"You think?" Mike said.

"Right," I said. "Maybe."

He looked at me. It was the morning after I'd phoned him from Chloe's Beetle, and we were on the middle landing of the cramped, winding captain's stairs that led down to the Millwood Inn's rear entrance. Or up to the second and third floors, depending on which direction you might be going.

"You're sure Kennedy's downstairs?" Mike asked in a low voice.

I nodded.

"I saw him in the common room," I said. "When I told Marge I was here to do my cleaning, he was at the buffet table with the rest of the guests."

"And there's no chance he noticed you?"

"None."

"Absolutely?"

I nodded my head.

"I stayed out of the room, Mike. His back was to me. And there were about twenty other people milling around the table, clacking dishes, clinking cups, and talking to each other."

"Then we shouldn't be having second thoughts," Mike said. "The coast's clear."

I hesitated. "Mike, the truth is Kennedy hasn't threatened me. We have no proof he's done anything wrong, except maybe park on the wrong side of the street."

"Outside the Fog Bell."

"Well, yes."

"Early yesterday morning."

"Yes . . . "

"Where he happened to zoom off the moment you left the house. And then seemed to be following you everywhere around town the *rest* of yesterday morning, to the point where you phoned me in a panic."

I paused uncertainly again, looked at him.

"We could tell Chief Vega what's happened," I said. "He could check out the suite."

"Not till he danced around legalities long enough to tip Kennedy off," Mike said. "Before Vega could get inside, he'd need a warrant. And to get a warrant he'd have to show some judge reasonable cause. And while Vega might very well feel that Kennedy's behavior toward you has been unusual, he'll have a hard time persuading the court of it."

"How do you know, Mike?"

"Because I've covered clear-cut stalking cases where the necessary threshold wasn't met in spite of overt physical and verbal intimidation," Mike said. "Like you told me, Kennedy has done no violence to you. He's said nothing overtly menacing. Vega doesn't have a single piece of concrete evidence to wave at anyone who could grant permission for a search."

"But it's okay for us to do it?"

"You have every reason to be in the room. Or any room in the inn. Your job is to clean them. And it's normal for you to have access when the guests are out."

"But I don't even have my bag of tricks with me," I said, hefting the ugly green metal toolbox Mike had dug out of his trunk. "Look at this thing. You've got nothing in it besides a few greasy rags and a wrench."

Mike gave a small smile.

"Beg your pardon," he said. "Some of those rags are unused. And there's also a pressure gauge and a tire patch kit."

"I'm serious, Mike. We're taking a big chance. And even if I have an excuse for being in the room, how about you?"

Mike looked at me, shrugged.

"That's just it," he said, and pressed a finger to his lips. "I'm not here."

I waited there a moment, my eyes on his. Then I sighed relentingly.

"Okay," I said. "We'd better hurry."

A couple of minutes later I let us into Old Abe's—no, I couldn't think of it that way, not anymore—make that *Adam Kennedy's* suite upstairs on the second floor. I stood behind the door, edging slightly to the left of it and leaving it open a crack so I could keep watch.

Mike, meanwhile, had gotten a digital camera out of his sport jacket and was moving around the place inspecting things. I didn't watch him too closely. I knew it would only make me anxious, and I figured I'd be better off focusing my attention on the hallway. But every now and then I'd look around and see him sorting through the contents of a drawer or a travel bag and snapping away.

"How much time will you need?" I said, glancing over my shoulder at him after what seemed like a long while.

"As much as I can have," Mike said. The camera's display screen in front of his face, he'd bent over some scattered papers on a table. Click, click, click. "Kennedy must plan on coming back upstairs after breakfast. He left his wallet behind. All sorts of identification. I've got shots of his driver's license, credit cards . . . stuff that should be easy to check out."

I took a deep breath to settle myself. And another. Then I turned back around toward the partially open door, standing at an angle that gave me a clear, unhindered view of the outer hall and master staircase.

It also put me right in line to see the antique

walnut stand on the right side of the door. To be perfectly accurate, it was a Queen Anne card table that must have been three hundred years old if it was a day . . . and Kennedy had left a half-filled glass of water on it. He hadn't bothered with a coaster, and I could already see a ring of moisture forming on the wood around the bottom of the glass.

Going to ruin the veneer, I thought. That and a floral inlay that some long-gone artisan must have spent months lavishing attention on. Workmanship that had kept its delicate beauty for centuries . . . and that Kennedy's glass of water was about to damage, maybe beyond repair.

Shades of the Slobby Bunch.

Under the circumstances, I suppose most people would have left the glass alone. I *knew* it probably wasn't the best moment for my cleanliness reflex to kick in—but I couldn't resist. Leaving that glass of water where it was would've been like being a willing bystander at an accident. You have to help when you can. And in this case, all I had to do was lift a glass off a table.

My right hand on the doorknob, I reached for the glass with my left. It remained slightly beyond my grasp, and I leaned across the door as far as I could, my feet planted, my arm stretched to the limit, trying to get my fingers around the glass while making sure I didn't budge from my lookout position.

I almost had it. So very *almost* that I could feel its smooth, curved surface in my fingertips.

And then it slipped right out from between them.

For a split second, I thought I'd be able to make up for my bobble and catch it. But then I was clutching nothing but air, and the glass fell down to the hardwood floor, and then shattered with a crash, splashing water everywhere.

"Sky, what the hell was that?"

This was Mike from behind me.

I whirled around and stared at him aghast, unable to say anything for a second, my eyes and mouth big, wide circles.

"Sky?"

"I broke the glass!" I said at last, managing to pry my tongue from where it had stuck to the roof of my mouth. "Oh, no, Mike, I broke the glass!"

He looked at me across the room.

"This is bad," he said.

"Worse than bad!"

"Worse?"

"Much worse," I said. "The common room's right underneath us."

"You think Kennedy might've heard?"

I nodded, gaped down in horror at sharp jags of glass lying strewn in a puddle on the floor. Then I raised my head and frantically looked back and forth. There was a towel hanging over the back of a chair outside the bathroom. I lunged across the room for it, snatching it off the chair, then darting back to kneel over the jumbled shards near the front door.

"Sky, what are you doing?" Mike said.

"Cleaning!" I slapped the towel over the puddled water to soak some of it up, then spread it open and hurriedly began picking up the jagged pieces of glass from the floor, setting them inside the towel, doubling it over them to form a sort of pouch.

"Sky, listen. Forget that. We have to get out of here. And I mean now."

I shook my head.

"If I don't get rid of the mess, Kennedy will know we were in the room."

Mike shook his head.

"No," he said rapidly. "He'll know *somebody* was in the room. But he won't know it was the two of us, not if we're gone before he—"

Mike stopped talking.

I made a stunned gasping sound that could have been mistaken for someone inhaling through a harmonica.

We'd both heard the heavy thump of footsteps out in the hall. They were coming toward the room, and coming fast.

Mike took a giant step toward me, reaching for my hand, wanting to help me to my feet. I grabbed hold of his hand and started to get up from my crouch.

And then the door slammed open, pushed open from outside, knocking into me hard and bouncing me right back down onto my rear end.

Suddenly Adam Kennedy came charging into

the room. He was wearing a knitted V-neck polo shirt with a light windbreaker over it, the jacket unzipped.

My first flickering thought was that it was a neat, casual spring look. My second—and this one screamed through my head—was that it was a convenient way to hide the pistol he'd whipped from somewhere under the windbreaker, gripping it in his fist, pointing it straight down at where I was sprawled on my backside.

"Don't make a sound," he said. "Do that, either of you, and you're both dead. My friend Sky here first."

Mike and I were quiet. He had a gun, and we didn't. That made his threat one to take seriously. And neither of us wanted to die.

Kennedy shuffled into the room, palmed the door shut behind him, and looked around, his gun steady in his hand.

"Get up and move over next to your friend there," he said to me, gesturing with the pistol. "Now."

I did, the barrel of the gun moving with me. It was some sort of automatic. I knew that not because I'm a firearms expert. But I'd seen enough TV shows and movies, and it didn't have a cylinder like a revolver.

"It seems like there isn't too much trouble in the world for these four walls to hold," Kennedy said, staring at me. "And you're always blowing in right at the head of it, aren't you?"

I stood beside Mike, my heart racing.

Kennedy flashed his glacial smile.

"Aren't you?" he repeated.

Still with that stare.

I tried to answer, but couldn't manage to get out a sound.

"This isn't her fault," Mike said. "She didn't want to come here. I forced her into it."

Kennedy's eyes flashed at him.

"That so?" he said.

Mike nodded.

"Yes," he said.

"No," I said, finding my voice.

"Don't listen to her," Mike said.

"Don't listen to him," I said.

Mike looked at me. I looked back at him.

"What are you doing?" he said.

"Telling the truth," I said.

"I'm trying to get you out of this, Sky."

"We're in it together, Mike."

"Shut your mouths, both of you," Kennedy said.

We were quiet. Again, so you don't forget, he was the one holding a gun.

Kennedy moved his eyes to my face.

"You know all about messes, don't you?" he said. "Well, this sort of mess isn't supposed to happen. I'm a professional, and I like doing things nice and neat." He grinned. "You believe me?"

I didn't say anything, terrified.

Kennedy made a kind of winding gesture with the gun.

"I asked you a question, Miss Clean Freak," he said. "I want an answer."

I swallowed. All at once, to my own amazement, I was not only scared but *furious*.

"If neat is leaving an old man dead on the floor, then I guess that's what you are," I heard myself say.

Kennedy's eyes held steady on me.

"He wouldn't have died if he'd been smart," he said. "I caught Skibaldi by surprise in here, same way I caught you. But instead of admitting who he was, he insisted his name was Monahan. Like I was going to believe that. Like I hadn't been on his tail for months. Like Mr. Navarro didn't have pictures of him, and like we couldn't use one of those computer programs that showed exactly how he'd look after thirty years." Kennedy paused. "You follow me so far?" he said.

I looked at him.

"Answer," he said.

"I follow you," I said.

Kennedy nodded.

"I didn't come to kill Skibaldi," he said. "He'd told me what I needed to know, I'd have left him in the closet with his cat and been on my way. But instead he starts tussling with me, falls against the bed, and bashes open his head. And then you make the situation even more complicated. Make a mess of everything."

I blinked, pointed to myself.

"Me?" I said. "How did I make—"

"If you hadn't come along, I'd have had a chance to look around this place. Find the thing that I wanted and that Skibaldi wouldn't give up.

But then I hear you cleaning that rug outside, and I have to stand here hoping you don't walk in on me. If you'd come into the room, I might have had to kill you on the spot. Good thing you ran downstairs for some reason."

To get the bag of ice cubes, I thought. *The ones I used to harden up the Gummi Bear.*

"Soon as you were gone, I took off. And talk about messes . . . I was out of here so fast, I didn't have a chance to wash away the blood that got on me," Kennedy went on. "Didn't realize it was on my hands till I see my fingerprints on the wall, where I was kind of leaning to see if you were coming back up those stairs." He stared at us, sending icy darts into my heart. "The same stairs you two must have walked up to sneak in here. The stairs we're all three going to go down together about minute from now."

"No," Mike said.

Kennedy's eyes went to his face.

"No?"

"No," Mike repeated. "Just take me with you. She stays. You know she won't talk as long as I'm your hostage."

I looked at Mike.

"Oh, no, you don't," I said.

"Yes, I do."

"Don't."

"Do."

"Don't," Kennedy snapped.

We looked at him.

"If anyone's useless to me, it's you, hero," he

said to Mike. "We're having ourselves a party here, we might as well be upfront with each other. All three of us know I came for the Brinks money. All three of us know Skibaldi buried it somewhere in Pigeon Cove. And at least one of us knows— or has a pretty good idea—where it is." His gaze shifted over to me, his smile tightening at the corners. "I've done my homework, Miss Clean Freak. I've talked to people about you all around this stinking nowhere town. My gabby hostess Marge, for one. That guy who sells snail puke for coffee. The jerk who owns the bookstore. Lots of other people. What I heard from them is that Skibaldi had a special twinkle for you. That he'd spend hours and hours talking to you alone. The more I heard from them, the more I wondered why any good-looking woman your age would waste your time with that dried-up fossil—and the only reason that made sense was the loot. Once I figured that out, everything else fell into place."

"You're wrong," I said. "Abe and I were friends. I didn't know about any money."

"I'll bet. That's why you cleaned this room and packed all his belongings into your car. Out of pure friendship, huh?"

I nodded.

"It's the truth," I said. "You can believe it or not."

Kennedy was no longer smiling at all.

"Don't give me that load," he said. "I wasn't born yesterday. You have yourself a new boyfriend here. Somebody who isn't decrepit like Skibaldi. Somebody who can put a smile on your face while sharing in the bucks." He paused. "Problem is, I've some thoughts of my own on that score, Miss Clean Freak. Because we're all going for a drive out to Maplewood Park together. And once we're there, you'll tell me where to find the Brinks loot. And if you don't, remember that the quarries are deep, and two bodies weighted down with those granite stones can stay sunk a long, long time before anybody finds them."

Something fell together for me then. I could almost hear the click in my head.

"Like my Toyota?" I thought aloud, and instantly wished I could yank the words back out of the air. But spoken or unspoken, it was a guess I'd have stuck with. Kennedy was the one who stole the SUV. He'd taken it so he could go through the cartons of Abe's belongings. And afterward he'd driven it over the side of the quarries. That would have made sense, if he was in a hurry to get rid of it and afraid the police dragnet would catch him if he tried leaving Cape Ann.

Kennedy looked at me, his gaze locking on mine.

"Let's go," he said. "Toward those back stairs."

"You're out of your mind," Mike said. "If you do this, it'll be for nothing. We don't know where the money—"

Kennedy waggled his pistol toward the door.

"Shut up and get moving," he said. "*Now*, or I swear I'll kill you both right here on the spot."

Mike and I shut up and moved. I suppose we

could have argued some more, but it was one of those times when you really don't have a whole lot of leverage.

We went out into the hallway and turned toward the captain's stairwell, Kennedy right behind us, his gun stuffed into the pocket of his windbreaker. All the while I was hoping somebody would come upstairs and find us, though part of me knew better than to expect it. Yes, I know, Kennedy had done it when he heard the glass break. He'd have had a reason. But nobody else would care about the noise, not while they were busy smacking their lips over Marge's scrumptious buffet items, not in time to interrupt what was happening.

We'd reached the end of the hall now, Kennedy's hidden gun still pointed at our backs.

"You start down first," he said to Mike. "Then you, Cleaning Witch."

I hesitated only a beat, and then jolted with fright. Kennedy had stepped up close so that his body was practically against me, the gun muzzle in his jacket pocket pressed into my spine.

"That's just so you don't forget where I am," Kennedy said. "Let's go."

And then we were in the stairwell, descending in single file, Kennedy and his gun a step above and behind me. We took a couple of sharp twists, some steep turns, and then were halfway down to the bottom, the screen door I'd repaired for Marge last month only a few feet below us, light streaming in from the backyard through which we'd soon be walking to Kennedy's white Nissan, and from there heading off to our de . . .

I never finished the terrible thought. My eye had touched on something just below me, resting on the little sill beneath the handrail. One of my bamboo skewers. I'd been using it to scrape dirt from the risers the other day and must have accidentally left it behind.

That didn't matter, though. Nothing did, except that it was there.

An idea flashed through my mind. A scary, dangerous idea. I had no time to falter, no time to think about the consequences of screwing up. I could either act or not.

And in the space of a heartbeat I did act, shooting a hand out toward the skewer, snatching it off the sill, and jabbing it backward into Kennedy's thigh as hard as I could.

I'll never forget the cry that left his lips, *never*— that or the sudden mixture of fear and desperate hope I felt as the skewer sank into his leg and he started wobbling on the step behind me, his foot slipping out from under him while he continued howling in pain and shock.

The rest happened in a blur. As Kennedy stumbled, I could feel his weight shift against me, and I sort of reacted without thinking, just really wanting to get out from under him—a move that, though I didn't realize it at the time, was about the best I could have made, since it made him completely lose his balance.

Only thing about that in hindsight: It would

have been a lot neater if I could've started a *controlled* fall.

His feet kicking in the air, arms flailing, Kennedy flipped over my back and went barreling down into Mike, who—give him loads of credit—had the presence of mind to grab hold of Kennedy as he *also* lost his footing and started to tumble downstairs.

And then I was screaming at the top of my lungs, shouting for somebody, *any*body to please come help us while the two of them spilled end over end down the steps, grabbing and punching each other as they fell, continuing to fight even after they'd landed in a heap at the bottom, Kennedy on top of Mike, Mike struggling to get out from under him, their arms and legs in a crazy, thrashing tangle.

I stood there a moment, not knowing what to do besides keep yelling my head off . . . and probably would have stayed right where I was in shrill, utter cluelessness if I hadn't seen Kennedy's hand fumbling for his jacket pocket.

The gun, I thought with sudden horror.

Kennedy was reaching for the gun.

Still screaming, I raced down the stairs just as he managed to yank it out of his pocket, his fist gripping . . . well, whatever they call the part of a gun you grip when you're going to shoot it at a person. Somehow I got both my hands around the thing, trying to wrench it out of his fingers from behind.

But Kennedy was stronger than I was, a whole

lot stronger, and I couldn't tear it away from him. And between my pulling it one way, and his pulling it another, and the trigger being caught between our violently opposing tugs, the gun did what guns are meant to do and fired with a deafening bang, its discharged bullet smashing into the ceiling above the stairs, sending a powdery shower of plaster down over everything.

I think that was when I became aware of the commotion from inside the house. Or maybe I actually heard it sooner—with all the confusion that was going on, it's hard to put certain things in the order they happened. But what I can guarantee is that a moment or two after the gunshot, Marge Millwood and her inquisitive breakfast crew appeared in the kitchen entry, shoving en masse toward the stairwell, crowding around us with their buttered rolls, coffee cups, and, in the case of the bigger eaters, plates of scrambled eggs and bacon, waffles, or French toast.

"Oh, my!" Marge said. She poked her head into the stairwell, a half-eaten cruller in her hand.

I remember seeing Kennedy roll partially off of Mike to stare upward at her in momentary distraction, the plaster dust on his hair and face making him look like a crazed, very befuddled ghost.

The next thing I remember is Mike's fist connecting with his face. And I do mean connecting. So hard it raised a whitish cloud of plaster around Kennedy's head.

Kennedy made a kind of snorting sound—the best I can describe it is *"Aguuchh!"*—then slumped backward on the floor, looking up into my face for one last bleary second before his eyes rolled up in their sockets and shut.

Though I'll never be sure, I don't believe he was thinking pleasant thoughts about me.

"Mike, are you all right?" I said, helping him to his feet. He was entirely coated in plaster.

"I am," he said, looking at me. "Sky, you saved my life."

I shook my head no.

"I think you saved mine, Mike."

"No, seriously," he said. "When you think about the whole situation, you saved my—"

"Sky, what in heaven's name happened to poor Mr. Kennedy?" Marge interrupted—and thankfully so, or we might still be there arguing about who saved whom.

I didn't answer. Not for a minute or two, anyway. I was dusting plaster out of my hair, looking up at the rather large bullet hole in the ceiling, and having a brainstorm.

A little toothpaste should keep it from getting any wider till it can be properly patched, I thought.

Chapter 15

" 'A smart, beautiful and shipshape young woman, you were like the daughter I never had.' " Mike was reading aloud.

He heard me clear my throat and looked up from the handwritten note I'd handed him.

"You okay, Sky?" he said, slipping off his newly repaired reading glasses.

I nodded from across the table and reached for my water.

"Fine," I said, drinking from the glass.

We were at Linaria in Gloucester, waiting for the dessert we'd never gotten around to having before our dinner date was aborted. This was Mike's idea. He'd wanted to make up for having botched things the first time around and had even promised that his aunt Ruthie would bake some sort of special chocolate fudge cake for the occasion.

I hadn't needed the added enticement. I didn't know where my relationship with Mike was heading—so much had happened to me lately, I hadn't had a chance to think about it. But thinking about it probably wasn't what I needed to do anyway. Whatever it was, or might or might not become, it wasn't something I could reason out by fitting one piece of a puzzle together with the next. I knew I liked Mike. I knew I was attracted to him. And I knew we were comfortable together as friends. Beyond that, I recognized that it was an open-ended question. All I could do was let myself go with what seemed right from moment to moment, and day to day, and try to be aware of my feelings. If I did that, I had a hunch things would come together on their own.

Mike slowly lowered the sheet of paper I'd handed him. It had arrived via Abe Monahan's attorney after about a thousand different sets of law enforcement people had searched his Florida home—a notarized, handwritten will that left me Skiball, a small monthly stipend to cover her care and feeding, and his parcel of land at the south end.

"It's still hard to believe," I said. "The person I knew as Abe Monahan was someone named Tony Skibaldi. And Frank Kennedy was Knuckles Navarro. Two sweet men who were really gangsters."

"Or gangsters who were really sweet," Mike said.

I looked at him.

"Seriously, Mike. You think that both can be true of them?"

He shrugged.

"People are complicated . . . not too many of us are ever one thing or the other," he said. "If there's a hard-core badguy here it's Adam Kennedy—a.k.a. Les 'Steel Eyes' Nittles, from the Windy City. Navarro never told his so-called nephew to harm Abe or anybody else. He just wanted the heist money."

"And loved dogs," I said.

"Like Abe loved his cat," Mike said. His eyes met mine over the flickering candle on the table between us. "And loved you."

I sat there for a long moment, feeling vaguely self-conscious.

"I'm not sure that 'love' is the word I'd use," I said.

Mike shrugged, returned Abe's will to me. "I don't know what else he could have meant, saying you were like a daughter to him. It's obvious that his scrub lot and Skiball were all he truly held precious. All he'd made provisions for in the event of his death. And he chose you as their caretaker."

I took a deep breath and slipped the will back into my purse. Never mind self-conscious; now I was embarrassed.

"Speaking of the lot . . . did the authorities really think Abe hid all the Brinks money there?" I said, wanting to change the subject.

Mike nodded.

"They still do. Never mind that they found barely a third of it buried in the ground," he said. "The feebs theorize Abe's stonewalling was exactly what it seemed to be. A hobby. Or maybe something to do with all the rocks he was digging up. It was easier than hauling them off, or leaving them in plain sight to possibly attract someone's curiosity. If you buy into their theory, he buried the loot in separate bundles that he planned to unearth one at a time."

"As he'd spend it over the years."

"Right." Mike looked at me. "You look skeptical."

"I am," I said. "I mean, the police turned that land upside down. But what happened to the money they *didn't* find? We're talking about a fortune, Mike. But from everything we know about Abe, he lived very modestly."

Mike was quiet. We both were. From around us at other tables came the soft clink of silverware on dishes, the low murmur of dinner conversation.

"Complicated," Mike said after a few seconds. "That goes for people *and* life in general. Maybe Abe had more secrets than anybody suspected . . . say, a bunch of different identities. Or could be the authorities are wrong and he stashed the rest of the loot somewhere else. We may never find out."

I let my mind hang on that thought for a moment.

"In the crime novels my friend Chloe devours, all the loose ends are neatly tied up before the story's over. But I suppose it's never like that in the real world, is it?"

Mike was watching me again in the candlelight.

"As I see it, the occasional loose end keeps us wondering, and that's not the worst thing," he said, his eyes on mine. "Sometimes, when one's tied up, I take it as a happy surprise."

He smiled a little mysteriously and then glanced over his shoulder. I looked too. I thought I'd heard Uncle Alex's voice, and I was right. He'd appeared from the kitchen with our waiter, the two of them wheeling a serving cart toward our table. On it was a tray covered with a large silver lid.

"Seems our soufflés are arriving in style," Mike said.

I looked at him.

"Our cake, you mean."

"What?"

"You'd said your aunt baked a special chocolate cake."

Mike blinked. "Oh. I guess I must've made a mista—"

"Here we are, kids!" Uncle Alex announced as the waiter finished pushing the cart over and hurried off. "Hope you're ready for Ruthie's delicious tarts."

"Tarts?" I said.

"Right, fruit tarts," Uncle Alex said. He exchanged a quick glance with Mike. "Isn't that what you told her?"

"I think I said it'd be a soufflé. And then revised that to a cake."

"Actually, you said cake first, and soufflé second," I reminded him.

Uncle Alex frowned at Mike.

"It was fruit tarts," he said. "We decided on fruit tarts."

Mike put his hand on his brow, shook his head.

"Sorry, you're right, it's tarts. I don't know why I keep getting confused."

Uncle Alex was still frowning at him.

"My nephew, the reporter who can't get a story straight," he said crossly. "Now I look dumb because of you."

I sat there a moment, figuring I'd better settle things down before Mike and Uncle Alex got into a full-blown family fracas.

"A cake, tarts, soufflés . . . they're all great," I said to Uncle Alex. "I can't wait to taste *whatever* it is."

He hovered over the cart, his frown inverting into an enormous grin.

"Now there's the right attitude, Skyros," he said. "This is why I keep saying you're a wonderful girl . . ."

"Uncle Alex," Mike said. "Maybe you ought to go ahead and show her the dessert."

Uncle Alex looked at him.

"Now?" he said.

"Would be perfect timing," Mike said.

They looked at each other for another second, then at me. And as I sat there looking back at them and wondering if we'd manage to get to our dessert sometime this century, Uncle Alex nodded, his hand going to the lid and lifting it from the tray.

My mouth fell open, and I let out a gasp.

"My bag of tricks," I said, snapping my head around toward Mike. "How—?"

"A couple of Chief Vega's men turned it up in Maplewood Park," he said. "Kennedy—Nittles, that is—must have searched through your SUV before ditching it in the quarry. I guess he didn't find anything useful to him and just tossed the bag into the woods."

I looked at him, my eyes wide with astonishment, my heart leaping around in my chest. And then, as I turned toward Uncle Alex again, he took the bag off the tray and turned it over to me with a flair usually reserved for the presentation of a coveted prize or trophy.

Until my fingers were actually around it, I think a big part of me—maybe even most of me—had withheld buying into the idea that it was for real. I was somehow imagining this whole episode. Or it was a different bag. I hadn't wanted to be disappointed.

But it was nothing I'd needed to worry about.

The bag was empty, and scuffed, and badly soiled, but that didn't make the slightest bit of difference.

It was my bag of tricks.

My one and only bag of tricks.

For real.

"Mike—" I swallowed hard and clutched the bag against my breast, too overwhelmed to articulate the thought rushing through my head.

Which was fine, because Mike managed to do it for me.

"One loose end happily tied up," he said.

Sky Taylor's Top Ten Cleaning Kit Items (and Tips on How to Use Them!)

1. Rubber Gloves

Rather than using standard yellow gloves when you clean, pick up a pair that's one of the new bright colors, like purple or hot pink. They'll be easy to spot and you won't be likely to leave them behind when you're done.

2. White Cleaning Cloths

I prefer the inexpensive terry-cloth washcloths. Before putting them in your kit, fold them once and then roll them into a cylindrical shape. You can then stack them standing up in your tote for easy access. They're great for when you use cleaning sprays, as well as for dusting and giving a

final wipe to chrome sinks and faucets. P.S.—
Don't forget the doorknobs!

3. *The Three-in-One*

This kit-within-a-kit is made up of about half a
dozen bamboo skewers, a paint scraper, and a paring knife. Again, I suggest you choose bright colors in the case of the last two items so they're
easier to spot. Use the skewers for small jobs, especially if you're picking or scraping grime from
a surface you don't want to scratch. They're also
great for hard-to-reach kitchen areas—say, spear-
ing bits of food that may have fallen into the space
between a stove and a butcher block. The paint
scraper's a good all-around tool for removing any
sticky goo or grimy buildup. And a paring knife
is not only cheap, it's also the sharpest, thinnest
blade you'll find with a handle. What's it for?
You'll know when you need it. Whether you use
it for cleaning blobs of dried paint or grime skirt-
ing the burners of your stove, believe me, you'll
know. Usually I leave the little cardboard sleeve
on the blade when it isn't in use—that keeps it
clean and sharp!

4. *Spray-Bottle Cleansers*

Don't get carried away stuffing your kit with
them. A window cleaner, a degreaser (if you're
doing the kitchen), and a green cleaner are more

than enough for almost any job. Everything else is redundant.

5. *A Roll of Paper Towels*

Or more accurately, a half-used roll. It's a pain lugging around those massive full rolls, and you won't need them. Paper towels are mostly for emergencies—pet accidents, cleaning clogged drain traps, or picking up dead bugs. As a rule, stick with your cleaning cloths whenever you do general tidying-up; they work a lot better.

6. *Scrub Brush and Toothbrush*

Use the larger scrub brush for ground-in dirt and scuff marks on the floor or other large surfaces. The toothbrush works great in tight corners, getting in between ceramic tiles, and around the base of faucets.

7. *Sponge (With an Abrasive Side)*

For sinks, counters, and appliances.

8. *Plastic Trash Bags*

Grocery bags are best for several reasons. One, they're thin, so you can fold several of them into your kit. Two, you can hang the full bags on doorknobs as you move from room to room, then collect them all at the same time when you're finished cleaning. And three—they don't cost you a cent!

9. Fels-Naptha Soap

A heavy-duty laundry bar soap that can remove just about every type of stain—and is easier to carry than a liquid detergent.

10. Cleaning Dough

Available at any good hardware store. If you don't already know how this can be used, you've skipped the rest of the book!

From the next book in the
Grime Solvers mystery series
Dirty Deeds
Coming from Signet in June 2008

"Our guests are the *loveliest*. I wish they'd leave," Chloe Edwards said, her snowflake earrings sparkling in the glow of the exhibit hall's overhead fluorescents.

I looked at her, a tray of drained and half-empty wineglasses balanced in my hands. On my last visit to my ex–flower child parents' house, I'd hid out for awhile, browsing the New Age section of their personal library. Besides reeking of patchouli incense, it takes up most of their shelf space, and is the place to go if you're eager to be schooled in alternative medicine, dream interpretation, holistic diets, chakras, channeling, and yes, Tantric sex therapy—there are loads and loads of books on that subject. But considering that we happen to be talking about my sixtyish mom and dad here, and that I'd rather not fall back on my old habit of grinding my teeth, I'd think I'd better truck on down to my major point, if you don't mind.

Said point being that I'd read a little about Zen

koans while thumbing through one of their books. As I understand it, these are riddles that defy rational solutions. A Buddhist teacher will relate a koan to his student, and the student will meditate on it and try to extract profound meaning from what seems superficially meaningless. The general idea is to open the mind to new insights and ways of thinking.

Which is pretty much what it's like interpreting Chloe-speak. What she'd said seemed to contradict itself, sure. But if you knew Chloe like I do, you'd realize that it didn't in the least. Chloe is actually the sharpest and most insightful person I know, and most of what leaves her lips makes good sense. You just need to put yourself in a Chloe state of mind to catch it.

Standing beside her in the large exhibit room on the ground floor of the Art Association building, I took a quick head count of the stragglers around us and then glanced at the people filing out the door.

"We're doing okay," I whispered. "Pretty much everybody has left."

Chloe checked her wristwatch and frowned a little. "That won't cut it, Sky. It's almost eleven o'clock at night, and my invitation clearly says the exhibit runs till ten. You can't finish tidying up until the last of them goes home."

I couldn't argue. It *was* getting late, and I was going to have my hands full getting everything done. But when Chloe had offered me the job of doing cleanup for that evening's event, I'd felt compelled to accept, never mind that I already had my hands full with the huge number of local inns holding Christmas and New Year's functions. I mean, let's be honest. My newspaper column's fun, but it isn't as though I can exactly pay my bills on the cup of coffee I'm paid for writing it. Also, I knew Chloe had gone out of her way to finagle the gig for me, and I didn't want to seem unappreciative, considering that her gala was the most prestigious—and best-paying— hobnob in town.

In Pigeon Cove, it's a seasonal tradition for the Art Association to hold a themed holiday bash about a week before Christmas, with a different member of the board of trustees selected to hostess the affair each year. This year it was Chloe's turn, and she'd done a bang-up job—especially considering that a group of the town's most influential businesspeople had lobbied for the exhibit to be given the anything-but-artful title "Pigeon Cove's Growth and Expansion in the Coming Year." They'd also done their best to turn the whole wingding into a shameless promotion for various moneymaking projects they had in the works.

Those hotshots hadn't reckoned with Chloe, though. Our local entrepreneurs may have intended to slap poster ads disguised as fine art prints all over the gallery walls, but she'd outsmarted them. If Chloe was going to be stuck with their commercial pitches—and she'd known she would be—she'd at least arranged to have the final word on the event's creative mode, insisting they use life-sized, three-dimensional multimedia dioramas to qualify. Her stipulation had made some genuine imagination flow from their mental taps, forced them to hire legit artists and craftspeople for the displays, and turned what could have been a long, tedious night into something that was really enjoyable.

Still, I could see Chloe starting to fade after mixing with the guests for hours. I sometimes had to remind myself she was only human, tireless as she seemed.

"Chloe, you don't have to say good night to every last comer," I said. "Since I've got to wait around anyway, you can leave it to me. . . ."

Chloe shook her head. "You're too easygoing, dear." She glanced over toward the appetizer table. "Look at the Fontaines still eating away! They're overstaying their welcome at your expense."

"Maybe so. But I can't exactly start pushing them out the door."

Chloe's finger snapped up to her chin like an exclamation point.

"No, you can't," she said. "That's the hostess's job, isn't it?"

And with that, she started toward a group of admirers lingering by the elaborate Getaway Grove Condominiums exhibit, which featured a stone path, a flower garden, and even a "snoozing" condo owner on a hammock, in the person of Kyle

Fipps. A third-generation real estate developer and wannabe actor, Kyle was one of Bill Drecksel's two major partners in a deal to build a number of fancy condo units at the South End. To the amusement of the viewers around him, he'd apparently gotten carried away with his role and fallen asleep in the display's mock spring gardens, a straw hat over his face.

I quickstepped in front of Chloe now, afraid she'd startle him into tipping off the hammock.

"Seriously," I said. "How about we give it a few minutes before we shoosh people off?"

Chloe hesitated a second, then released a sigh.

"All right," she said. "Provided I stay here and help you clean."

I frowned. Besides the gigantic snowflake earrings dangling almost to her shoulders, Chloe had on a bright, Christmassy red silk tunic with matching slim pants and heels, not quite your usual cleaning uniform. Of course, neither was my foxy pleated black minidress, red-and-white Santa hat, or color-splashed vintage Peter Max scarf I was wearing courtesy of Mom. But I'd had to put on something decent while picking up after the guests, and had brought a smock in my bag of tricks—that's what I call my cleaning kit—for when I got around to the heavy-duty scrubbing.

"Chloe, don't be ridiculous," I said. "I can take care of things on my lonesome."

Chloe made a stubborn face, her lips pursed. "I'm sure that's true. But as long I'm here, you won't. Or must I remind you we're supposed to be best fr—" She suddenly broke off and looked over my shoulder. "Why, hello, Finch."

"*Salut*," Finch said from behind me. "I hope I'm not interrupting an important conversation."

"Not really. I'd just been thinking about how much hard work Sky has ahead of her." Chloe gave Finch a stiff smile. "She can't get started until everyone leaves."

I turned to look at Finch, who'd carried a plate over from the appetizer table. She seemed oblivious to Chloe's implication.

"You know, I honestly cannot decide whether I prefer the *foie gras* or the *pâté de volaille*, they're both so delicious," Finch said, and popped a morsel of pricey finger food into her mouth. "Although I enjoyed sampling those delectable *beignets de fromage* while the warm appetizers were being served."

Chloe and I stood there in abashed silence. A minuscule woman of about forty-five, with a thin waifish face, sandy brown hair, and soft brown eyes, Finch preferred being called Miss Finch by her dance students at the Fontaine Culture Club, which she'd cofounded with her husband, Alexander, and was touting as a premier center for the advancement of modern dance and song on Cape Ann. To hear Finch tell it, she'd pulled the club together entirely with her own blood, sweat, and tears—the same way she boasted of having made herself a top-notch dancer by working twice as hard as everyone else in the world. Never mind that her biggest claim to fame was having been featured in a Billy Idol video in the mideighties; forget that the Fontaine Culture Club had been financed using her generous family trust fund; and put aside the fact that its board of directors set up the whole thing as a tax write-off while she and Alexander were away on an extended photographic safari in West Africa.

"So, Chloe, tell me how you felt about my exhibit," Finch said now.

"I enjoyed it," Chloe said. "It was very clever."

"And brilliantly executed, don't you agree?"

Chloe looked at her, took a deep breath. "I can see that a great deal of planning went into it, yes."

"Planning and vision," Finch chirped. "The motif came to me in a burst of inspiration so powerful I was left breathless. It's sui generis. Alone, apart, to itself."

Chloe's mouth tightened again. I knew she was anxious not to offend Finch. For all her preening and pretense, Finch was a staunch patron of the Art Association. And I had to admit that her exhibit for the Culture Club *was* inventive enough. Stepping up to a large window frame, you were given a simulated glimpse into the building's main practice studio, where dozens of Barbie dolls were twirling in tights and tutus. Symbolically outside the window, meanwhile, was a tree full of battery-operated finches that would flap their little wings, and open and close their beaks in time to various pieces of music playing from camouflaged speakers.

"Finch, I'd love to compliment you some more, but I want to show Sky a few things that need to get done around here," Chloe said pleasantly. She smiled without evident sarcasm. "Also, I believe there's heavy snow in tomorrow's forecast. You might want to get a jump on it heading home."

I bit my lip. A jump? The Fontaines lived right around the corner from the Art Association, and Chloe was well aware of it. But I was hoping Finch would take the unsubtle hint.

It turned out she did. Either that, or she'd grown bored with us. It was impossible to tell, and I honestly didn't care as she bade us *bonne nuit* and *au revoir*, and then went to separate her husband from the picked-over remnants of the appetizers.

Chloe watched them head toward the coatroom.

"Self-praise is no praise at all," she whispered to me.

"Got that right," I said, my eyes going to the front entrance.

It looked as though people had at long last decided to call it an evening. Possibly, I thought, they'd taken a cue from the Fontaines. But whatever the reason, the exhibit hall had entirely emptied out within minutes after Finch and Alexander left.

Well, okay. It had *almost* emptied.

Glancing around the room, I realized that Morris Silverberg, the ophthalmologist, was still hanging out at his Presbiopic Bocci Ball Court, stuffing a cannoli into his mouth with one hand and adjusting some of the eyeglass frames hanging from the exhibit's giant Christmas tree with the other. But at least Morris had on his winter parka and seemed ready to make tracks.

Unfortunately the same couldn't be said for Kyle Fipps. Over at the Getaway Grove display, he was still out like a light, the straw hat covering his face.

I poked Chloe with my elbow, nodded in his direction.

"Can you believe the guy?" I said. "That's what I call taking performance art to a new level."

Chloe shook her head thoughtfully.

"It could be," she said. "Of course, I did notice him sampling the wine before. The poor man's been going through that terrible divorce with his wife, Lina. . . . It could be that he had a bit too much to drink."

I looked at her.

"You think our happy hammock snoozer's *plotzed*?"

Chloe shrugged.

"I don't know," she said. "We'd better check on him."

As we crossed the room to the exhibit, I realized I was still holding the tray of dirty glasses and unsuccessfully looked around for a place to set it down. At the same time, Chloe went walking up the stone path to the hammock and gave it a gentle push.

Kyle didn't stir.

"Kyle," Chloe said quietly. "Rise and shine."

He still didn't move.

Chloe glanced at me, her brow creasing.

"What do you think?" I said.

"I think I'd better treat him to a cheerful little wake-up ditty."

I shrugged, tray in hand. Crazy as it sounds, Chloe's idea didn't surprise me. For that matter, it was fairly routine coming from her.

She turned back toward Kyle, leaned close to his ear, and then started singing about Dorothy the dinosaur munching on some roses and Wag the dog digging up bones.

It didn't work. Kyle remained absolutely still.

Chloe had gotten around to the part of the song where Henry the octopus was doing something or other in circles when I decided to walk up the path and give her an assist. Maybe, I thought, Kyle needed a bit more than a kid's song and a tender nudge to get him moving.

"C'mon, Kyle! Nap time's over. Let's go!" I said in a loud voice, lifting the hat off his face while balancing my tray in one hand.

I looked down at him, my jaw suddenly dropping.

Kyle's eyes were open. I mean, *wide* open. And glassy. And his face was a very deep and disconcerting shade of purple.

Standing over him, Chloe screamed, and that was what set off the chain reaction: her scream startling me into dropping the tray, wineglasses spilling from the tray into the fake garden grass. The next thing I knew, Chloe had kind of bumped into the hammock, and Kyle had fallen over its side to the floor, dropping heavily amid the strewn glasses and plastic potted plants, sprawling there in a motionless heap.

"Coming through! I'm a doctor!" It was Silverberg the eye specialist, thudding over from his indoor bocci court. He stood over the body and looked at me. "Does that man need a doctor?" he asked.

I looked back at Silverberg. All things considered—and my dropped tray aside—I felt fairly composed. But, then, this wasn't the first time I'd stumbled onto a dead body.

"Something tells me Kyle won't be needing any more eye tests, Morrie," I said.

About the Author

Suzanne Price is the pseudonym for a nationally bestselling author. While Suzanne has never solved a murder, she's as quick with cleaning hints as her heroine.

Kate Collins

The Flower Shop Mystery Series

Abby Knight is the proud owner of her hometown flower shop. She has a gift for arranging flowers—and for solving crimes.

Acts of Violets
Mum's the Word
Slay It with Flowers
Dearly Depotted
Snipped in the Bud

"A spirited sleuth, quirky sidekicks,
and page-turning action."
—Nancy J. Cohen